12·32

DEGENERATION
AND
REGENERATION

TEXTS OF
THE PREMODERN ERA

A TWENTY-NINE-VOLUME FACSIMILE SERIES
REPRESENTING THE HIGHLY VARIED
CULTURAL THEMES OF THE 1890S IN
PROSE AND POETRY

EDITED BY
IAN FLETCHER &
JOHN STOKES

GARLAND PUBLISHING

MODERN INSTANCES

Ella D'Arcy

Garland Publishing, Inc., New York & London

1984

For a complete list of the titles in this series
see the final pages of this volume.

This facsimile has been made from a copy in
the British Library.

828
D214mo

Library of Congress Cataloging in Publication Data

D'Arcy, Ella.
Modern instances.

(Degeneration and regeneration)
Reprint. Originally published: London :
J. Lane, Bodley Head, 1898.
I. Title. II. Series.
PR6007.A522M6 1984   823'.8   82-49094
ISBN 0-8240-5552-7 (alk. paper)

85-2130

The volumes in this series are printed on
acid-free, 250-year-life paper.

Printed in the United States of America

Modern Instances

By the same Author

MONOCHROMES

THE BISHOP'S DILEMMA

Modern Instances

BY

ELLA D'ARCY

JOHN LANE: The Bodley Head
LONDON & NEW YORK
1898

CONTENTS

AT TWICKENHAM

A

AT TWICKENHAM

WHEN John Corbett married Minnie Wray, her
sister Lœtitia, their parents being dead, came to
live under his roof also, which seemed to Corbett
the most natural arrangement in the world, for
he was an Irishman, and the Irish never count
the cost of an extra mouth. "Where there's
enough for two, there's enough for three," is a
favourite saying of theirs, and even in the most
impecunious Irish household no one ever dreams
of grudging you your bite of bread or your sup
o' th' crathur.

But Corbett was not impecunious. On the contrary, he was fairly well off, being partner in and
traveller for an Irish whisky house, and earning
thus between eight and nine hundred a year. In
the Income Tax returns he put the figure down
as five hundred, but in conversation he referred
to it casually as over a thousand; for he had
some of the vices of his nationality as well as
most of its virtues, and to impress Twickenham

with a due sense of the worth of John Corbett
was perhaps his chief preoccupation out of business hours.

He lived in an imitation high art villa on the
road to Strawberry Hill ; a villa that rejoiced in
the name of "Braemar," gilded in gothic letters
upon the wooden gate ; a villa that flared up into
pinnacles, blushed with red-brick, and mourned
behind sad-tinted glass. The Elizabethan case-
ments let in piercing draughts, the Brummagem
brass door-handles came off in the confiding
hand that sought to turn them, the tiled hearths
successfully conducted all the heat up the chimneys
to disperse it generously over an inclement sky.
But Corbett found consolation in the knowledge
that the hall was paved with grey and white
mosaic, that "Salve" bristled at you from the
door-mat, that the dining-room boasted of a dado,
and that the drawing-room rose to the dignity of
a frieze.

Minnie Corbett, whose full name was Margaret,
but who preferred to be called Rita, although she
could not teach her family to remember to call
her so, and Lœtitia, who had recently changed
the "Tish" of her childhood to the more poetical
"Letty," dressed the windows of "Braemar" with
frilled Madras muslin, draped the mantel-pieces
with plush, hung the walls with coloured photo-
graphs, Chinese crockery, and Japanese fans.

They made expeditions into town in search of pampas grass and bulrushes, with which in summer-time they decorated the fireplaces, and in winter the painted drain-pipes which stood in the corners of the drawing-room.

Beyond which labours of love, and Minnie's perfunctory ordering of the dinner every morning, neither she nor Lœtitia found anything to do, for Corbett kept a cook, a house-parlourmaid, and two nurses to look after Minnie's three children, in whom her interest seemed to have ceased when she had bestowed on them the high-sounding names of Lancelot, Hugo, and Guinevere. Lœtitia had never pretended to feel any interest in the children at all.

The sisters suffered terribly from dulness, and one memorable Sunday evening, Corbett being away travelling, they took first-class tickets to Waterloo, returning by the next train, merely to pass the time.

When Corbett was not travelling, his going to and fro between Twickenham and the City lent a spice of variety to the day. He left every morning by the 9.15 train, and came home in the evening in time for a seven o'clock dinner. On Saturdays he got back by two, when he either mowed the lawn in his shirt-sleeves, or played a set of tennis with Lœtitia, or went with both girls for a row on the river. Or, if Minnie made a special point of it, he escorted them back into town, where he treated them to a restaurant *table d'hôte* and a theatre afterwards. On Sundays he rose late, renewed his weekly acquaintance with the baby, read through the *Referee* from first line to last, and accompanied by his two little boys dressed in correct Jack Tar costume, went for a walk along the towing-path, whence they could watch the boating.

Humanly speaking, he would have liked to have followed the example of those flannel-shirted publicans and sinners who pushed off every moment in gay twos and threes from Shore's landing-stage, but consideration for the susceptibilities of Providence and of Twickenham held him in check.

It is true he did not go to church, although often disquieted by the thought of the bad effect this omission must produce on the mind of his next-door neighbour; but he salved his conscience with the plea that he was a busy man, and that Sunday was his only day of home life. Besides, the family was well represented by Minnie and Lœtitia, who when the weather was fine never missed morning service. When it was wet they stayed away on account of their frocks.

Sunday afternoons were spent by them sitting in the drawing-room awaiting the visitors who did not come. The number of persons in Twickenham with whom they were on calling terms was limited, nor can it be maintained that " Braemar" was an amusing house at which to call. For though Corbett was one of the most cordial, one of the most hospitable of young men, his women-folk shone rather by their silences than by their conversational gifts.

Minnie Corbett was particularly silent. She had won her husband by lifting to his a pair of blankly beautiful eyes, and it did not seem to her requisite to give greater exertion to the winning of minor successes.

Lœtitia could talk to men provided they were unrelated to her, but she found nothing to say to members of her own sex. Even with her sister she was mostly silent, unless there was a new fashion in hats, the cut of a sleeve, or the set of a skirt to discuss. There was, however, one other topic which invariably aroused her to a transitory animation. This was the passing by the windows in his well-appointed dog-cart, of a man whom, because of his upright bearing, moustache, and close-cut hair, she and Minnie had agreed to call "the Captain."

He was tall, evidently, and had a straight nose. Lœtitia also was straight-nosed and tall. She saw in this physical resemblance a reason for fostering a sentimental interest in him.

"Quick, Minnie, here's the Captain!" she would cry, and Minnie would awake from the somnolency of Sunday with a start, and skip over to the window to watch a flying vision of a brown horse, a black and red painted cart, and a drab-coated figure holding the reins, while a very small groom in white cords and top-boots maintained his seat behind by means of tightly folded arms and a portentous frown.

"He's got such a pretty horse," observed Minnie on one occasion, before relapsing back into silence, the folding of hands, and a rocking-chair.

"Yes," Lœtitia agreed pensively, "it has such a nice tail."

Although she knew nothing concerning the Captain, although it did not seem probable that she ever would know anything, although it was at least a tenable supposition that he was married already and the father of a family, she saw herself, in fancy, the wife of the wearer of the drab coat, driving by his side along the roads of Twicken-ham, up the High Street of Richmond. She wore, in fancy, a sealskin as handsome as Minnie's and six inches longer, and she ordered lavishly from Gosling and the other tradesmen, giving the address of Captain Devereux of Deepdene, or Captain Mortimer of the Shrubberies. The names were either purely imaginary, or remini-

scent of the novels she constantly carried about
with her and fitfully read.

She sat nearly always with an open book upon
her knee, but neither Hall Caine nor Miss Marie
Corelli even in their most inspired moments
could woo her to complete self-forgetfulness.
She did not wish to forget herself in a novel.
She wished to find in it straw for her own brick-
making, bricks for her own castle-building. And
if a shadow fell across the window, if a step was
heard along the hall, she could break off in the
most poignant passage to lift a slim hand to the
better arrangement of her curls, to thrust a slim
foot in lace stocking and pointed shoe to a position of greater conspicuousness.

On Sunday evenings at "Braemar" there was
cold supper at eight, consisting of the early
dinner joint, eaten with a salad scientifically
mixed by Corbett, the remains of the apple or
gooseberry pie, cheese, and an excellent Bur-
gundy obtained by him at trade price. When
the cloth was removed he did not return to the
drawing-room. He never felt at ease in that
over-furnished, over-ornate room, so darkened by
shaded lamps and pink petticoated candles that it
was impossible to read. The white, untempered
flames of three gas-burners in the dining-room
suited him better, and here he would sit on one
side of the hearth in an armchair grown comfort-

able from continual use, and read over again the already well-read paper, while Minnie, on the other side of the hearth, stared silently before her, and Lœtitia fingered her book at the table.

Sometimes Corbett, untaught by past experience, would make a hopeful appeal to one or the other, for an expression of opinion concerning some topic of the day; the last play, the newest book. But Minnie seldom took the trouble to hear him at all, and Lœtitia would answer with such superficial politeness, with so wide an irrelevance to the subject, that, discouraged, he would draw back again into his shell. At the end of every Sunday evening he was glad to remember that the next day was Monday, when he could return to his occupations and his acquaintances in the City. In the City men were ready to talk to him, to listen to what he said, and even to affect some show of interest in his views and pursuits.

The chief breaks in his home life, its principal excitements, were the various ailments the children developed, the multifarious and unexpected means they found of putting their lives in jeopardy and adding items to Dr. Payne's half-yearly accounts. Corbett would come home in the happiest mood, to have his serenity roughly shattered by the news that Lancelot had forced a boot-button down his ear, and was rolling on the

floor in agony; that Hugo had bolted seventeen cherry-stones in succession and obstinately
refused an emetic; that the baby had been
seized with convulsions; that the whole family
were in for chicken-pox, whooping-cough, or
mumps.

On such occasions Minnie, recovering something of her antenuptial vivacity, seemed to take
a positive pleasure in unfolding the harrowing
details, in dwelling on the still more harrowing
consequences which would probably ensue.

When, on turning into Wetherly Gardens on
his way from the station, Corbett perceived his
wife's blonde head above the garden gate, he
knew at once that it betokened a domestic
catastrophe. It had only been in the very early
days of their married life that Minnie had hurried
to greet his return for the mere pleasure it gave
her.

The past winter had brought rather more than
the usual crop of casualties among the children,
so that it had seemed to Corbett that the parental
cup of bitterness was already filled to overflowing,
that Fate might well grant him a respite, when,
returning from town one warm May Saturday, his
thoughts veering riverwards, and his intention
being to invite the girls to scull up and have tea
at Tagg's, his ears were martyrised by the voci-
ferous howls of Hugo, who had just managed to

pull down over himself the kettle of water boiling on the nursery fire.

While the women of the household disputed among themselves as to the remedial values of oil, treacle, or magnesia, Corbett rushed round to Payne's to find him away, and to be referred to Dr. Matheson of Holly Cottage, who was taking Payne's cases. At the moment he never noticed what Matheson was like, he received no conscious impression of the other's personality. But when that evening, comparative peace having again fallen upon the Villa, Lœtitia remarked for the twentieth time, " How funny that Dr. Matheson should be the Captain, isn't it ? " he found in his memory the picture of a tall fair man, with regular features and a quiet manner, he caught the echoes of a pleasantly modulated voice.

The young women did not go to service next morning, but Lœtitia put on her best gown nevertheless. She displayed also a good deal of unexpected solicitude for her little nephew, and when Matheson looked in, at about 11 A.M., she saw fit to accompany him and Corbett upstairs to the night-nursery, where Minnie, in a white wrapper trimmed with ribbons as blue as her eyes and as meaningless, sat gazing into futurity by her son's bedside.

Hugo had given up the attempt to obtain illuminating answers to the intricate social and

ethical problems with which he wiled away the
pain-filled time. For when by repeated interro-
gatives of "Mother?" "Eh, mother?" "Well,
mother?" he had induced Minnie at least to listen
to him, all he extracted from her was some
unsatisfying vagueness, which added its quota to
the waters of contempt already welling up in his
young soul for the intelligence of women.

He rejoiced at the appearance of his father and
the doctor, despite some natural heart-sinkings as
to what the latter might not purpose doing to
him. He knew doctors to be perfectly irresponsible autocrats, who walked into your bedroom,
felt your pulse, turned you over and over just as
though you were a puppy or a kitten, and then
with an impassive countenance ordered you a
poultice or a powder, and walked off. He knew
that if they condemned you to lose an arm or a
leg they would be just as despotic and impassible,
and you would have to submit just as quietly.
None of the grown-ups about you would ever
dream of interfering in your behalf.

So he fixed Matheson with an alert, an inquiring,
a profoundly distrustful eye, and with a hand in
his father's, awaited developments. Lœtitia he
ignored altogether. He supposed that the existence of aunts was necessary to the general scheme
of things, but personally he hadn't any use for
them. His predominate impression of Auntie

Tish was that she spent her day heating curling-irons over the gas-bracket in her bedroom, and curling her hair, and although he saw great possibilities in curling-irons heated red-hot and applied to reasonable uses, he was convinced that no one besides herself ever knew whether her hair was curled or straight. But women were such ninnies.

The examination over, the scalds re-dressed and covered up again, Matheson on his way downstairs stopped at the staircase window to admire the green and charming piece of garden, which ending in an inconspicuous wooden paling, enjoyed an illusory proprietorship in the belt of fine old elm trees belonging to the demesne beyond.

Corbett invited him to come and take a turn round it, and the two young men stepped out upon the lawn.

It was a delicious blue and white morning, with that Sunday feeling in the air which is produced by the cessation of all workaday noises, and heightened just now by the last melodious bell-cadences floating out from the church on the distant green. The garden was full of flowers and bees, scent and sunshine. Roses, clematis, and canariensis tapestried the brick unsightlinesses of the back of the house. Serried ranks of blue-green lavender, wild companies of undisciplined sweet pea, sturdy clumps of red-hot poker shooting up in fiery contrast to the wide-spreading luxuriance of the cool white daisy bushes, justled side by side in the border territories which were separated from the grass by narrow gravel paths.

While Corbett and his guest walked up and down the centre of the lawn, Minnie and Lœtitia watched them from behind the curtains of the night-nursery window.

" He's got such nice hands," said Lœtitia, " so white and well kept. Did you notice, Minnie ? " Lœtitia always noticed hands, because she gave a great deal of attention to her own.

But Minnie, whose hands were not her strong point, was more impressed by Matheson's boots. " I wish Jack would get brown boots, they look so much smarter with light clothes," she remarked, but without any intensity of desire. Before the short phrase was finished, her voice had dropped into apathy, her gaze had wandered away from Matheson's boots, from the garden, from the hour. She seemed not to hear her sister's dubious " Yes, but I wonder he wears a tweed suit on Sundays ? "

Lœtitia heard herself calling him Algernon or Edgar, and remonstrating with him on the sub-ject. Then she went into her bedroom, recurled a peccant lock on her temple, and joined the men just as the dinner gong sounded.

Matheson was pressed to stay and share the early dinner. " Unless," said Corbett, seeing that

he hesitated, "Mrs. Matheson . . . perhaps . . .
is waiting for you ?"

"There is no Mrs. Matheson, as yet," he
answered smiling, "although Payne is always
telling me it's my professional duty to get married
as soon as possible."

Lœtitia coloured and smiled.

.

From that day Matheson was often at
"Braemar." At first he came ostensibly to attend
to Hugo, but before that small pickle was on his
feet again and in fresh mischief, he was sufficiently
friendly with the family to drop in without any
excuse at all.

He would come of an evening and ask for
Corbett, and the maid would show him into the
little study behind the dining-room, where Corbett
enjoyed his after-dinner smoke. He enjoyed it
doubly in Matheson's society, and discovered he
had been thirsting for some such companionship
for years. The girls were awfully nice, of course,
but . . . and then, the fellows in the City . . . he
compared them with Matheson, much to their
disadvantage. For Matheson struck him as being
amazingly clever—a pillar of originality—and his
fine indifference to the most cherished opinions
of Twickenham made Corbett catch his breath.
But the time spent with his friend was only too

short. Minnie and Lœtitia always found some pretext to join them, and they would reproach Matheson in so cordial a manner for never coming into the drawing-room, that presently, somewhat to Corbett's chagrin, he began to pay his visits to them instead.

Then as the summer advanced, the fine weather suggested river picnics, and the young women arranged one every week. They even ventured under Matheson's influence to go out on a Sunday, starting in the forenoon, getting up as far as Chertsey, and not returning till late at night. Corbett, half delighted with the abandoned devilry of the proceeding, half terrified lest Wetherly Gardens should come to hear of it, or Providence deal swift retribution, was always wholly surprised and relieved when they found themselves again ashore, as safe and comfortable as though the day had been a mere Monday or Wednesday. And if this immunity from consequences slightly shook Corbett's respect for Providence, it sensibly increased his respect for his friend.

Corbett would have enjoyed this summer extremely, but for the curious jealousy Minnie began to exhibit of his affection for Matheson. It seemed to him it could only be jealousy which made her intrude so needlessly on their *tête-à-têtes*, interrupt their conversation so pointedly, and so frequently reproach Corbett, in the privacy of the

B

nuptial chamber, for monopolising all the attention of their guest.

"You're always so selfish," Minnie would complain.

Yet, reviewing the incidents of the evening — Matheson had been dining perhaps at " Braemar " —it seemed to Corbett that he had hardly had a chance to exchange a word with him at all. It seemed to Corbett that Lœtitia had done all the talking; and her light volubility with Matheson, so different from the tongue-tiedness of her ordinary hours, her incessant and slightly meaningless laugh, echoed in his ears at the back of Minnie's scoldings, until both were lost in sleep.

But when the problem of Minnie's vexation recurred to him next morning, he decided that the key to it could only be jealousy, and he was annoyed with himself that he could find no excuses for a failing at once so ridiculous and so petty. The true nature of the case never once crossed his mind, until Minnie unfolded it for him one day, abruptly and triumphantly.

"Well, it's all right.   He's proposed at last."

"What do you mean ? Who ?" asked Corbett bewildered.

"Why Jim Matheson, of course ! Who else do you suppose ?   He proposed to Tish last night in the garden. You remember how long they were out there, after we came in ?   That was why."

Corbett was immensely surprised, even incredulous, although when he saw that his incredulity made his wife angry, he stifled it in his bosom.

After all, as she said with some asperity, why shouldn't Matheson be in love with Lœtitia? Lœtitia was a pretty girl . . . a good girl . . . yet somehow Corbett felt disappointed and depressed.

" You're such a selfish pig," Minnie told him ; " you never think of anybody but yourself. You want to keep Tish here always."

Corbett feared he must be selfish, though scarcely in respect to Lœtitia. In his heart he would have been very glad to see her married. But he didn't want Matheson to marry her.

" Jim's awfully in love," said Minnie, and it sounded odd to Corbett to hear his wife call Matheson " Jim." " He fell in love with her the very first moment he saw her. That's why he's been here so often. You thought he came to see you, I suppose ? "

Her husband's blank expression made her laugh.

" You *are* a pig ! " she repeated. " You never do think of any one but yourself. Now hurry up and get dressed, and we'll go into town and dine at the Exhibition, and after dinner we'll go up in the Big Wheel."

" Is Letty coming too ? " Corbett asked.

" Don't be so silly ! Of course not. She's expecting Jim. That's why I'm taking you out.

You don't imagine they want your society, do you ? Or mine ? " she added as an afterthought, and with an unusual concession to civility.

Henceforward Corbett saw even less of Matheson than before. He was as fond of him as ever, but the friendship fell into abeyance.

It seemed too that Matheson tried to avoid him, and when he offered his congratulations on the engagement, the lover showed himself singularly reticent and cold. Corbett concluded he was nervous. He remembered being horribly nervous himself in the early days of his betrothal to Minnie Wray, when her mother had persisted in introducing him to a large circle at Highbury as " My daughter Margaret's *engagé.*"

On the other hand, Corbett could not enough rejoice at the genial warmth which the event shed over the atmosphere of " Braemar." Both young women brightened up surprisingly, nor was there any lack of conversation between them now. Corbett thankfully gathered up such crumbs of talk as fell to his share, and first learned that the wedding was to take place in October, when Minnie informed him she must have a new frock. She rewarded him for his immediate consent by treating him to a different description of how she would have it made, three nights in the week.

Lœtitia thought of nothing but new frocks, and set about making some. A headless and armless

idol, covered in scarlet linen, was produced from
a cupboard, and reverentially enshrined in the
dining-room. Both sisters were generally found
on their kness before it, while a constant chatter-
ing went on in its praise. Innumerable yards of
silk and velvet were snipped up in sacrifice, and
the sofas and chairs were sown with needles and
pins, perhaps to extract involuntary homage from
those who would not otherwise bow the head.
The tables were littered with books of ritual having woodcuts in the text and illuminated pictures
slipped between the leaves.

There were constant visits to Richmond and
Regent Street, much correspondence with milliners
and dressmakers, a long succession of drapers'
carts standing in the road, of porters laden with
brown paper parcels passing up and down the
path. Lœtitia talked of Brighton for her wedding
tour, and of having a conservatory added to the
drawing-room of Holly Cottage. Friends and
acquaintances called to felicitate her, and left to
ask themselves what in the world Dr. Matheson
could have seen in Letty Wray. Presents began
to arrive, and a transitory gloom fell upon
"Braemar" when Lœtitia received two butter
dishes of identical pattern from two different
quarters, neither of which, on examination by the
local clockmaker, proved to be silver.

In this endless discussion of details, it did occasionally cross Corbett's mind that that which might perhaps be considered an essential point, namely, Matheson's comfort and happiness, was somewhat lost sight of. But as he made no complaint, and maintained an equable demeanour, Corbett supposed it was all right. Every woman considered the acquisition of fallals an indispensable preliminary to marriage, and it was extravagant to look for an exception in Lœtitia.

Matters stood thus, when turning into Wetherly Gardens one evening at the end of August, Corbett perceived, with a sudden heart-sinking, Minnie awaiting him at the gate. He recited the litany of all probable calamities, prayed for patience, and prepared his soul to endure the worst.

"What *do* you think, Jack," Minnie began, with immense blue eyes, and a voice that thrilled with intensity. "The most dreadful thing has happened——"

"Well, let me get in and sit down at least," said Corbett, dispiritedly. He was tired with the day's work, weary at the renewal of domestic worry. But the news which Minnie gave him was stimulating in its unexpectedness.

"Jim Matheson's been here to break off the engagement! He actually came to see Tish this afternoon and told her so himself. Isn't it monstrous? Isn't it disgraceful? And the presents come and everything. She's in a dreadful state. She's been crying on the bed ever since."

But Lœtitia, hearing her brother-in-law's step in the hall, came downstairs, her fringe, ominous sign, out of curl, her eyes red, her face disfigured from weeping.

And when she began, brokenly, "He's thrown me over, Jack! He's jilted me, he's told me so to my face! Oh, it's *too* hard. How shall I ever hold up my head again?" then, Corbett's sympathy went out to her completely. But he wanted particulars. How had it come about? There had been some quarrel surely, some misunderstanding?

Lœtitia declared there had been none. Why should she quarrel with Jim when she had been so happy, and everything had seemed so nice? No, he was tired of her, that was all. He had seen some one else perhaps, whom he fancied better, some one with more money. She wept anew, and stamped her foot upon the floor. "I wish you'd kill him, Jack, I wish you'd kill him!" she cried. "His conduct is infamous!"

Matheson's conduct as depicted by the young women did seem infamous to Corbett, and after the first chaotic confusion of his mind had fallen into order again, his temper rose. His Irish pride was stung to the quick. No one had a right to treat a woman belonging to him with contumely.

He would go up to Matheson, at once, this very evening, and ask him what he meant by it. He would exact ample satisfaction.

He swallowed a hurried and innutritious meal, with Lœtitia's tears salting every dish, and Minnie's reiterations ringing dirges in his ears. She and Lœtitia wanted him to "do something" to Matheson; to kill him if possible, to horsewhip him certainly. Corbett was in a mood to fall in with their wishes, and the justice of their cause must have seemed unimpeachable to them all, since neither he nor they reflected for a moment that he could not have the smallest chance in a tussle with the transgressor, who overlooked him by a head and shoulders, and was nearly twice his size.

This confidence in righteousness is derived from the story-books, which teach us that in personal combat the evil-doer invariably succumbs, no matter what the disparity of physical conditions may be; although it must be added that in every properly written story-book it is always the hero who boasts of breadth of muscle and length of inches, while the villain's black little soul is clothed in an appropriately small and unlovely body.

Corbett, however, set off without any misgivings.

He found Matheson still at table, reading from

a book propped up against the claret-jug. He refused the hand and the chair Matheson offered him, and came to the point at once.

" Is this true what I hear at home ? That you came up this afternoon to break off your engagement with Lœtitia ?"

Matheson, who had flushed a little at the rejection of his hand-shake, admitted with evident embarrassment that it was true.

" And you've the—the cheek to tell me that, to my face ?" said Corbett, turning red.

" I can't deny it, to your face."

"But what's your meaning, what's your motive, what has Letty done ? What has happened since yesterday ? You seemed all right yesterday," Corbett insisted.

" It's not Letty's—it's not Miss Wray's fault at all. It's my mistake. I've made the discovery we're not a bit suited to each other, that's all. And you ought to be thankful, as I am, that I've discovered it in time."

"Damn it !" exclaimed Corbett, and a V-shaped vein rose in the centre of his forehead, and his blue eyes darkened. " You come to my house, I make a friend of you, my wife and sister receive you into their intimacy, you ask the girl to be your wife. . . . I suppose you admit doing that ?" he interpolated in withering accents ; " and now you throw her away like an old glove, break her heart, and expect me to be thankful ?   Damn it all, that's a bit steep."

"I shouldn't think I've broken her heart," said Matheson, embarrassed again.   "I should hope not."   There was interrogation in his tone.

"She feels it acutely," said Corbett.   "Any woman would.   She's very——" he stopped, but Matheson had caught the unspoken word.

"Angry with me ?   Yes.   But anger's a healthy sign.   Anger doesn't break hearts."

"Upon my soul," cried Corbett, amazed at such coolness, "I call your conduct craven ! I call it infamous!" he added, remembering Lœtitia's own word.

"Look here, Jack," appealed the other, "can't you sit down ?   I want to talk the matter over with you, but it gets on my nerves to see you walking up and down the room like that."

Corbett, all unconscious of his restlessness, now stood still, but determined that he would never sit down in Matheson's house again.   Then he weakly subsided into the chair which his friend pushed over to him.

"You call my conduct craven?   I assure you I never had to make so large a demand upon my courage as when I called upon Lœtitia to-day.   But I said to myself, a little pluck now, a bad quarter of an hour to live through, and in all probability you save two lives from ruin. For we should have made each other miserable."

" Then why have engaged yourself ? " asked Corbett with renewed heat.

" Yes . . . why ? Do you know, Jack, that the very morning of our engagement, five minutes even before the fateful moment, I'd no more idea . . . but you know how such things can come about. The garden, the moonlight, a foolish word taken seriously . . . and then the apparent impossibility of drawing back, the reckless plunging deeper into the mire. . . . I don't deny I was attracted by Letty, interested in her. She is a pretty girl, an unusually pretty girl. But like most other girls she's a victim to her upbringing. Until you are all in all to an English girl you are nothing at all. She never reveals herself to you for a moment ; speaks from the lips only ; says the things she has been taught to say, that other women say. You've got to get engaged to a woman in England, it seems, if you're ever to know anything about her. And I engaged myself, as I told you, in a moment of emotion, and then hopefully set to work to make the best of it. But I didn't succeed. I didn't find in Letty the qualities I consider necessary for domestic happiness."

" But Letty is a very good——"

Matheson interrupted with " In a way she's too

good, too normal, too well-regulated. I could almost prefer a woman who had the capacity, at least, for being bad! It would denote some warmth, some passion, some soul. Now, I never was able to convince myself that Lœtitia was fond of me. Oh, she liked me well enough. She was satisfied with my position, modest as it is, with my prospects. My profession pleased her, principally as she confessed to me, that it necessitates my keeping a carriage. But *fond* . . . do you think she is capable of a very passionate affection, Jack?

"Of course, I know this is going to do me a lot of harm. Twickenham, no doubt, will echo your verdict, and describe my conduct as infamous. I daresay I shall have to pull up stakes and go elsewhere. But for me, it has been the only conduct possible. I discovered I didn't love her. Wouldn't it be a crime to marry a woman you don't love? I saw we could never make each other happy. Wouldn't it be a folly to rush open-eyed into such misery as that?"

Which was, practically, the end of the matter, although the friends sat long over their whisky and cigarettes, discussing all sublunary things. Corbett enjoyed a most delightful evening, and it had struck twelve before he set off homewards, glowing outside and in with the warmth which good spirit and good fellowship impart. He

reaffirmed to his soul the old decision that
Matheson was undoubtedly the cleverest, the
most entertaining, the most lovable of men—and
suddenly he remembered the mission on which he
had been sent nearly four hours ago ; simultane-
ously he realised its preposterous failure. All
his happy self-complacency radiated off into the
night. Chilled and sobered and pricked by conscience, he stood for a moment with his hand
upon the gate of " Braemar," looking up at the
lighted windows of Minnie's room.

What was he going to say to her and to
Lœtitia ? And, more perturbing question still,
what, when they should hear the truth, were his
womenfolk going to say to him ?

A MARRIAGE

A MARRIAGE

I

IN the upstairs room of a City restaurant two
young men were finishing their luncheon. They
had taken the corner table by the window, and
as it was past three o'clock the room was nearly
empty. There being no one at either of the
tables next them, they could talk at their ease.

West, the elder of the two, was just lighting a
cigarette. The other, Catterson, who, in spite of
a thin moustache, looked little more than a boy,
had ordered a cup of black coffee. When even a
younger man than he was at present, he had
passed a couple of years in Paris, and he continued, by the manner in which he wore his hair,
by his taste in neckties, and by his preferences
in food and drink, to pay Frenchmen the sincerest
flattery that was in his power.

But to-day he let the coffee stand before him
untasted. His young forehead was pushed up into

horizontal lines, his full-lipped mouth was slightly open with anxious, suspended breath. He gazed away, through the red velvet lounges, through the gilt-framed mirrors, to the distant object of his thought.

West, leaning back in his seat, emitting arabesques and spirals of brown-grey smoke, watched him with interest rather than with sympathy, and could not repress a smile when Catterson, coming abruptly out of dreamland, turned towards him, to say : "You see, if it were only for the child's sake, I feel I ought to marry her, and the next may be a boy. I should like him to inherit the little property, small as it is. And I've no power to will it."

His voice was half decided, wholly interrogative, and West smiled. There had been a moment in all their conversations of the past six weeks, when some such remark from Catterson was sure to fall. Experience enabled West to anticipate its arrival, and he smiled to find his anticipation so accurately fulfilled.

" My dear chap, I see you're going to do it," he answered, "so it's useless for me to protest any more. But I'll just remind you of an old dictum, which, maybe, you'll respect, because it's in French : ' Ne faites jamais de votre maîtresse, votre femme.' "

West spoke lightly, uttering the quotation just

because it happened to flash through his mind; but all the same, it was a fixed idea of his, that if you married a girl of "that sort," she was sure to discover, sooner or later, colossal vices; she was sure to kick over the traces, to take to drink, or to some other form of dissipation.

Catterson shrugged his shoulders, flushed, and frowned; then recovered his temper, and began again, stammeringly, tumultuously, his words tripping over one another in their haste. He always stammered a little in moments of emotion.

"But you d-don't know Nettie. She's not at all—s-she's quite different from what you think. Until she had the misfortune to meet with me, she was as good a girl as you could find."

"No, I don't know her, I admit," observed West, and smoked in silence.

"I have been thinking," Catterson said presently, "that I should like you to come down to see her. I should like you to make her acquaintance, because then I am sure you would agree I am right. I do want to have your support and approval, you know."

West smiled again. It amused him to note the anxiety Catterson exhibited for his approval and support, yet he knew all the time that the young man was bent on marrying Nettie Hooper in spite of anything he could say.

But he understood the springs of the apparent

contradiction. He understood Catterson fairly well, without being fond of him. They had been schoolmates. Chance lately, rather than choice on West's side, had again thrown them together; now the luncheon hour saw them in almost daily companionship. And, correcting his impressions of the impulsive, sensitive, volatile little boy by these more recent ones, he read Catterson's as a weak, amiable, and affectionate nature; he saw him always anxious to stand well with his associates, to be liked and looked up to by his little world. To do as others do, was his ruling passion; what Brown, Jones, and Robinson might say of him, his first consideration. It was because at one time Robinson, Jones, and Brown had been represented for him by a circle of gay young Frenchmen that he had thought it incumbent upon him, when opportunity offered, to tread in their footsteps. It was because he found his path set now within the respectable circles of British middle-class society, that his anomalous position was becoming a burden; that the double personality of married man and father in his riverside lodgings, of eligible bachelor in the drawing-rooms of Bayswater and Maida Vale, grew daily more intolerable to sustain. He could think of no easier way out of the dilemma than to make Nettie his wife, and to allow the news gradually to leak out that he had been married for the last two years.

Some of his arguments in favour of the marriage —and he required many arguments to outweigh his consciousness of the *mésalliance*—were, that for all practical purposes, he was as good as married already. He could never give Nettie up; he must always provide for her and the child as long as he lived. And his present mode of life was full of inconveniences. He was living at Teddington under an assumed name, and it is not at all pleasant to live under an assumed name. At any moment one may be discovered, and an awkward situation may ensue.

These were some of his arguments. But then, too, he had developed the domestic affections to a surprising degree, and if his first passion for Nettie were somewhat assuaged, he had a much more tender feeling for her now than in the beginning. And he was devoted to his little daughter; a devotion which a few months ago he would have sworn he was incapable of feeling for any so uninteresting an animal as a baby. He reproached himself bitterly for having placed her at such a disadvantage in life as illegitimacy entails; he felt that he ought at least to give the expected child all the rights which a legal recognition can confer.

His chief argument, however, was that he had sinned, and that in marriage lay the only reparation; and let a man persuade himself that a certain course of action is the one righteous, the

one honourable course to take and—more particularly if it jumps with his own private inclinations
—nothing can deter him from it.

" Not even French proverbs," laughed West into
his beard.

"Come down and see her," Catterson urged,
and West, moved by a natural curiosity, as well as
by a desire to oblige his friend, agreed to meet
him that evening at Waterloo, that they might go
down together.

His soul being eased by confession, Catterson
regained at once the buoyant good spirits which
were natural to him, but which, of late, secret
anxieties and perturbation of mind had overshadowed completely. For when depressed he
touched deeper depths of depression than his
neighbour, in exact proportion to the unusual
height and breadth of his gaiety in moments of
elation.

Now he enlivened the journey out from town,
by cascades of exuberant talk, filling up the in-
frequent pauses with snatches of love-songs : the
music-hall love-songs of the day.

Yet as the train approached Teddington, he fell
into silence again. A new anxiety began to
dominate him : the anxiety that West should be
favourably impressed by Nettie Hooper. His
manner became more nervous, his stammer increased ; a red spot burned on either cheek. He

could not keep his thoughts or his speech from the coming interview.

"She doesn't talk much," he explained, as they walked along the summer sunset roads; "she's very shy; but you mustn't on that account imagine she's not glad to see you. She's very much interested in you. She wants to meet you very much."

"Of course she's not what's called a lady," he began again; "her people don't count at all. She, herself, wants to drop them. But you would never discover she wasn't one. She has a perfect accent, a perfect pronunciation. And she is so wonderfully modest and refined. I assure you, I've known very few real ladies to compare to her."

He eulogised her economy, her good management. "My money goes twice as far since she has had the spending of it. She's so clever, and you can't think how well she cooks. She has learned it from the old lady with whom we lodge. Mrs. Baker is devoted to Nettie, would do anything for her, thinks there's no one like her in the world. And then she makes all her own clothes, and is better dressed than any girl I see, although they only cost her a few shillings."

He sang the praises of her sweetness, of her gentleness, of her domesticity. "She's so absolutely unselfish; such a devoted mother to our little girl; and yet, she's scarcely more than a child herself. She won't be nineteen till next April."

All which encomiums and dozens more wearied West's ear, without giving him any clear conception of their subject. He was thankful when Catterson suddenly broke off with, " Here we are, this is Rose Cottage."

West saw the usual, creeper-covered, French-windowed, sham-romantic, and wholly dilapidated little villa, which realises the ideal of all young lovers for a first nest. To more prosaic minds it suggested earwigs and spiders in summer, loose tiles and burst pipes in winter, and general dampness and discomfort all the year round.

It stood separated from the road by a piece of front garden, in which the uncut grass waved fairy spear-heads, and the unpruned bushes matted out so wide and thick as to screen the sitting-room completely from the passers-by.

The narrow gravel path leading up to the door was painted with mosses, the little trellis-work porch was giving way beneath the weight of vine-wood and rose-stem which lay heavy upon it ; the virginia-creeper over the window-top swayed down to the ground in graceful diminishing tresses; the bedroom windows above blinked tiny eyes beneath heavy eyelids of greenery. An auctioneer would have described the place as a

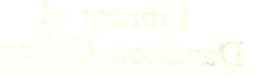

bijou bower of verdure, and West's sense of humour was tickled by the thoroughly conventional background it provided for the conventional *solitude à deux*.

Catterson rang that he might give notice of West's arrival, and a thin bell responded to his pull from the interior of the house. It was succeeded by the tapping of high heels along the oilcloth, the door opened, and a very little woman, in a dark woollen gown, stood within the threshold.

The nurse, the landlady, the servant, perhaps? West told himself that *this* could not be Nettie Hooper, this plain little creature, who was surely so much older than the girl Catterson had described.

But the next instant Catterson said, " Nettie, this is my great friend, West," and the little woman had given him a lifeless hand, while she welcomed him in curious, drawling tones, " I'm so glad to see you ; Jack is always talking about you ; do come in."

He was certain shè was plain, but he had no time to localise her plainness—to decide whether it lay in feature, complexion, or expression, for her back was now towards him ; he was following her into the sitting-room, and as he went he looked down upon a dark head of hair, a meagre figure, a dowdy home-made gown.

"I hope you've got a good dinner for us,"
Catterson began at once, stammering over
every consonant. "I don't know how West
may be feeling, but I'm uncommonly hungry
myself."

"You didn't give me much time," she answered;
"your wire only came at four. I've got you some
fish, and a steak."

"And a salad? Good! Nettie's steaks are
ripping, West, you'll see."

"Oh, but Mrs. Baker is going to cook the dinner
to-night. I didn't think you'd wish me to leave
you and Mr. West, like that."

During these not very illuminating remarks,
West was revising his first impressions. He
confessed that the girl had nice features, regular,
well-proportioned; that, though she lacked colour,
her complexion was of a healthy paleness; that
her expression could hardly be called disagreeable,
for the difficulty lay in deciding whether she had
any expression at all. All the same, she was not
pretty : and she was flat-chested, undeveloped, had
clumsy hands and feet.

"You have a—quiet little place here," he said
to her to make conversation. He had been going
to say "a charming little place," but a glance
round the dark, musty-smelling room was too
much for his powers of unveracity.

"Yes, it's almost too quiet, while Jack is away.

Don't you think, Mr. West, I'm very good to stay here by myself all day long ?"

She had the oddest voice, very drawling, very measured, quite inanimate. It said nothing at all to the listener beyond the mere actual words.

"Come, you've got baby," said Catterson, laughing, "let alone Mrs. Baker."

"As though one's landlady and a baby of seventeen months were all the companionship one could require !" She laughed too.

She was almost pretty when she laughed, and West began to perceive that after all she might be no older than Catterson had said. She had the abundant crisp-growing hair, the irreproachable smoothness of skin found only in youth's company. Her eyes were really remarkable eyes, large, of a bluish-grey, clear as water, with the pupils very big.

Yes, she was exceedingly pretty. It took you some time to see it perhaps, but once you had seen it you wondered you could have overlooked it before. Yet West had no sooner admitted the fact than he began to qualify it. He said there was absolutely nothing in her face that appealed to your imagination ; that such very limpid eyes go with a cold or a shallow nature, that such very large pupils denote either want of intelligence or want of strength.

And there was undeniably something common

in her physiognomy, although at first he could not decide in which particular trait it lay. Was it in the cut of the nostril, the line of the mouth ? No, he thought it was to be found, rather, in a certain unpleasing shininess of surface. Her cheek had less of the velvety texture of the peach, than the glaze of the white-heart cherry. The wings of the nose, its slightly aquiline bridge, reflected the light in little patches.

If her hair was unusually thick, it was coarse too, and of a uniform dark-brown colour. The front, cut short, seemed to rebel against the artificial curling to which it was subjected. Instead of lying on her forehead in rings as was no doubt intended, here was an undistinguishable fuzz, while there a straight mesh stood out defiantly.

She had pretty ears and execrably ugly hands, in the thick fingers of which, with squat nails broader than they were long, in the tough and wrinkled skin, the want of race of her ancestors was easily to be read. On the left hand she wore a plain gold ring.

So soon as the first fillip of greeting was spent, she became noticeable for her silences ; had a way of letting every subject drop ; and expressed no opinions, or only those universal ones which every woman may express without danger of self-revelation. For instance, when West asked whether she cared for reading, she said she was passionately fond of it ; but when pressed as to what she liked best to read, she mentioned, after considerable hesitation, " East Lynne " and " Shakespeare."

As Catterson had said, there was no fault to find with her pronunciation or her accent ; or what faults there were, were faults he himself was guilty of. West realised that she was quick in imitation, and, up to a certain point, receptive. She had carefully modelled her deportment on Catterson's, held her knife and fork, lifted her glass, and used her table-napkin in precisely the same way he did. When, later on, West had occasion to see her handwriting he found it a curiously close copy of Catterson's own. Women, whose characters are still undeveloped, and whose writing therefore remains unformed, almost invariably do adopt, for a time, the handwriting of their lovers.

There was nothing in her manners or appearance, to indicate her precise social origin, nor did West, by-the-by, ever learn anything definite concerning it. Catterson was very sensitive on the point, and only once made the vaguest, the most cursory reference to how he had met her.

Still less was there anything about Nettie Hooper to fit in with West's preconceived theories. As she sat there, placid, silent, quiet, he had to admit that as Catterson had said, she was not at all the sort of girl he had imagined her to be. And yet . . .

He made the above mental notes during the course of the dinner, while Catterson's nervousness gradually wore off, and his gaiety returned. His infatuation for Nettie, led him, when in her presence, to the conviction that every one else must be equally infatuated too.

The dining-room was small like the parlour, and looked out through a French window, over a tangled slip of garden. The furniture consisted chiefly of Japanese fans, but there was also a round table, and at least three chairs. The arrangements, generally, were of a picnic character, and when Mrs. Baker, a stout and loquacious old body, brought in the dishes, she stayed awhile to join in the conversation, addressing them all impartially as " My dear," and Nettie in particular as " My dear Life."

But the meal if simple, was satisfying, and Nettie herself left the table to make the coffee, as Catterson had taught her to do, in French fashion. He brought out from the chiffonier a bottle of green Chartreuse, and Nettie handed cigarettes and found an ash-tray. She was full of ministering attentions.

While they smoked and talked, and she sat silent, her limpid eyes fixed usually on Catterson, although every now and then, West knew they

were turned upon him, wails were heard from
upstairs.

"It's baby, poor little soul," said Nettie, rising.
" Please, Jack, may I go and bring her down ? "

She presently returned with a flannel-gowned
infant in her arms. The child had just the same
large, limpid, blue-grey eyes as the mother, with
just the same look in them. She fixed West with
the relentless, unswerving stare of infancy, and
not all her father's blandishments could extract a
smile.

Nettie, kissing the square-toed, pink feet, addressed her as "Blossom," and "Dear little soul;"
then sat tranquilly nursing her, as a child might
nurse a doll.

She had really many of a child's ways, and
when Catterson, at the end of the evening, put
on his hat to accompany West to the station, she
asked in her long, plaintive drawl, " May I come,
too, Jack ? " exactly as a child asks permission of
parent or master. She put her head back again
into the dining-room a moment after leaving it.
" What shall I put on, my cloak or my cape ? "
she said ; "and must I change my shoes ? "

Catterson turned to West with a smile, which
asked for congratulations. " You see how docile
she is, how gentle ? And it's always the same.
It's always my wishes that guide her. She never
does anything without asking my opinion and

advice. I don't know how a man could have a better wife. I know I should never find one to suit me better. But now you've seen her for yourself, you've come over to my opinion, I feel sure ? You've got nothing further to urge against my marrying her, have you ? "

West was saved the embarrassment of a reply by the reappearance of Nettie in outdoor things, and Catterson was too satisfied in his own mind with the effect she must have produced, to notice the omission.

He talked blithely on indifferent matters until the train moved out of the station, and West carried away with him a final vignette of the two young people standing close together beneath the glare of a gas-lamp, Catterson with an arm affectionately slipped through the girl's. His thin, handsome face was flushed with excitement and self-content. The demure little figure beside him, that did not reach up to his shoulder, in neat black coat and toque, stared at West across the platform, from limpid, most curious eyes.

What the devil was the peculiarity of those eyes, he asked himself impatiently ? and hammered out the answer to the oscillations of the carriage, the vibration of the woodwork, the flicker of the lamp, as the train rumbled through the night and jerked up at flaring stations.

Beautiful as to shape and colour, beautiful in

their fine dark lashes, in their thinly pencilled brows, these strange eyes seemed to look at you and ostentatiously to keep silence ; to thrust you coldly back, to gaze through you and beyond you, as if with the set purpose of avoiding any explanation with your own.

It was this singularity which in the shock of first sight had repelled, which had shed over the face an illusory plainness, which had suggested age and experience, so that it had taken West an appreciable time to discover that Nettie Hooper was in reality quite young, and exceedingly pretty. But he had learned on a dozen previous occasions, that the first instantaneous, unbiassed impression is the one to be trusted. Especially in so far as concerns the eyes. The eyes are very literally the windows of the soul.

II

THREE years later, West and two men who don't come into this story at all, were spending the month of August up the river. An ill-advised proceeding, for the weather, so far, had proved deplorably wet, as the weather in August too often does, and of all sad places in wet weather, the river is incomparably the saddest.

But they had hired their boat, they had made their arrangements, dates were fixed, and places decided on. With the thoroughly British mental twist that to change your plans is to show inconsistency, and therefore weakness, West's companions were determined to carry these plans out to their prearranged end.

He scoffed at their mulishness, but submitted nevertheless ; and following their example he rowed with bent head and set teeth through the continually falling rain, or sat in their society during interminable hours waiting for it to cease, in an open boat beneath a dripping elm-tree. And as he gazed out over the leaden sheet of pock-marked water, he found amusement in telling himself that here at least was a typically national way of taking a holiday.

Nor, after all, did it always rain. There were occasional days of brilliant, if unstable sunshine, when the stream ran dimpling between its banks of sweet flag and loosestrife; when the sand-martins skimmed across the water with their pitter-ing cry; when the dabchick, as the boat stole upon her, dived so suddenly, remained under for so long, and rose again so far off, that but for a knowledge of her habits, you would pronounce it a genuine case of bird suicide.

It was on one such a sunny, inspiriting Satur-day, that a twenty mile pull from Maidenhead brought them by afternoon in sight of the pic-turesque old bridge at Sonning. Here, in Son-ning, they were to pass the night and stay over till Monday. For here one of the men had an aunt, and he was under strict maternal orders to dine with her on Sunday.

There was the usual difference of opinion as to which of the two inns they should put up at, the White Hart being voted too noisy, the French Horn condemned as too swagger. But the ques-tion was settled by the White Hart, which you reach first on the Berkshire bank, proving full; they accordingly pulled round the mill-water on the right, to try their luck at the French Horn.

For those who do not know it, this may be described as one of the prettiest of riverside inns; a cosy-looking, two-storied house, with a wide verandah, and a lawn sloping down to the water's edge. Beneath the trees on either side, tea was set out on wicker tea-tables, and each table had its encircling group of gay frocks and scarlet sunshades. It presented a Watteau-like picture of light and shadow and colour, the artistic value of which was increased by three conspicuous figures, which took the spectator's eye straight to the centre of the foreground.

A man, a girl, and a little child stood together, just above the wooden landing-steps, and a Canadian canoe, brilliant with newness and varnish, flaring with flame-coloured cushions, rocked gently on the water at their feet.

The young man who held the painter in his hand, was dressed in immaculate white flannel, wore a pink and white striped shirt, and a waist-kerchief of crimson silk.

The girl was the boating-girl of the stage. Where the rushes fringed the lawn you looked instinctively for footlights. The open-work silk stockings, the patent leather evening shoes, the silver belt compressing a waist of seventeen inches, were all so thoroughly theatrical. So was her costume of pale blue and white; so was the knot of broad ribbon fastening her sailor collar;

so was the Jack Tar cap, with its blue and silver binding, set slightly on one side of her dark head. The child by her side was dressed in white embroidered muslin and a sun-bonnet.

"I say, West," cried the man who steered, "you who know all the actresses, tell us who's that little girl there, with the kid."

West, who was sculling, turned his head.

"Oh, damn! it's Mrs. Catterson," he said, with the emphasis of a surprise, which is a disagreeable one.

Since the marriage, he had not seen very much of Nettie Catterson, although he was godfather to the boy. For one thing, it is difficult to see much of people who live in the suburbs; and though Catterson had moved twice, first from Teddington to Kingston, then from Kingston to Surbition Hill, where he was now a householder, Surbition remained equally out of West's way.

But there was another reason for his evasion of the constant invitations which Catterson pressed upon him in the City. It had not taken him long to perceive that he was far from being *persona grata* to Mrs. Catterson. Whether this was to be accounted for by the average woman's inevitable jealousy of her husband's friends, whether it was she suspected his opposition to her marriage, or whether she could not forgive him for having known her while she was passing as Mrs. Gray, he could not determine. Probably her dislike was compounded of all three reasons, with a preponderance, he thought, in favour of the last.

For with marriage, with the possession of a semi-detached villa at Surbiton, and the entrance into such society as a visit from the clergyman's wife may open the door to, Nettie had become of an amazing conventionality, and surpassing Catterson himself in the matter of deference to Mrs. Grundy, she seemed to have set herself the task of atoning for irregularity of conduct in the past, by the severest reprobation of all who erred in the present; and West's ribaldry in conversation, his light views on serious subjects, and his habitual desecration of the Sunday, were themes for her constant animadversions and displeasure.

It was the rapid *résumé* of these, his demerits with Mrs. Catterson, which had called forth his energetic " Damn ! "

At the same moment that he recognised her, Catterson recognised him, and sung out a welcome. The boat was brought alongside, and he was received by Nettie with a warmth which surprised him. His companions, with hasty cap-lifting, escaped across the lawn to get drinks at the bar, and secure beds for the night.

He looked after them with envy, and found himself obliged to accept Nettie's invitation to tea.

"We were just quarrelling, Jack and I," she said, "where to have it. He wants to go down to Marlow, and I want it here. Now you've come, that settles it. We'll have it here."

Catterson explained his reason: as Nettie wished to go out in the canoe again, they ought to go now while it was fine, as it was sure to rain later.

Nettie denied the possibility of rain with an asperity which informed West that he had arrived on the crest of a domestic disagreement, and he understood at once the cordiality of his reception.

She had developed none of the tempestuous vices which his theories had required; on the contrary she appeared to be just the ordinary wife, with the ordinary contempt for her husband's foibles and wishes. She could talk of the trials of housekeeping and the iniquities of servants as to the manner born, and always imitative, had lately given back the ideals of Surbiton with the fidelity of a mirror. But there were curious undercurrents beneath this surface smoothness, of which West now and then got an indication.

He renewed his acquaintance with Gladys, the little girl, who periodically forgot him, and then asked after his godson. But the subject proved unfortunate.

Nettie's mouth took menacing lines. "Cyril,

I'm sorry to say, is a very naughty boy. I don't
know what we're going to do with him, I'm sure."

West could not help smiling. "It's somewhat
early days to despair of his ultimate improvement,
perhaps ? How old is he ? Not three till December, I think ?" He told himself that the open-
hearted, sensitive, impulsive little fellow ought not
to be very difficult to manage.

"He's old enough to be made to obey," she
said, with a glance at Catterson, which suggested
some contentious background to the remark.

"Oh, well, one doesn't want to break the child's
spirit," Catterson protested.

"I think his spirit will have to be broken very
soon," asserted Nettie, "if he goes on being as
troublesome as he has been lately."

Gladys, sitting by her mother's side, drank in
everything that was said. She was now five years
old, and a little miniature of Nettie. She turned
her clear and stolid eyes from one to another.

"Cyril's a . . . naughty . . . little boy," she
observed in a piping drawl, a thin exaggeration
of Nettie's own, and making impressive pauses
between the words. "He's never going to be
tooked . . . up the river like me. Is he, mother?"

"If you want to be a good little girl," observed
Catterson, "you'll put your bread and jam into
your mouth, instead of feeding your ear with it as
you are doing at present."

"Cyril don't have . . . no jam . . . for *his* tea," she began again, "'cos he's so naughty. He only has dry bread an'——"

"Come, come, don't talk so much, Gladys," said her father impatiently, "or perhaps you won't get 'tooked' up the river again either."

Nettie put an arm round her.

"Poor little soul! Mother'll take her up the river always, won't she? We don't mind what Papa says, do we?"

"Silly old Papa!" cried the child, throwing him one of Nettie's own looks, "we don't mind what he says, we don't."

All the same, when tea was over, and they prepared to make a start in the canoe, West their still somewhat unwilling guest, Catterson put his foot down and refused to take Gladys with them for various reasons. Four couldn't get into the canoe with safety or comfort; the child had been out all day, and had already complained of sickness from the constant swaying motion; but chiefly because it was undoubtedly going to rain. Nettie gave in with a bad grace, and the little girl was led off, roaring, by her maid.

Nettie had complained that the tea was cold, and that she could not drink it. She had insisted on Catterson having a second brew brought. Then when this came she had pushed away her cup, and pronounced it as unpalatable as the first.

But no sooner were they some way down stream, than she said she was thirsty, and asked for ginger beer.

West remembered Catterson telling him long ago, how Nettie would suddenly awake thirsty in the middle of the night, and how he would have to get up and go down to forage for something to quench her thirst. It had seemed to Catterson, in those days, very amusing, pathetic, and childlike, and he had told of it with evident relish and pride. But the little perversity which is so attractively provoking in the young girl, often comes to provoke without any attractiveness in the wife and mother.

Catterson turned the canoe when Nettie spoke, saying they had best go and get what she wanted at the White Hart, but West fancied he looked annoyed and slightly ashamed.

After this little episode, because of the ominous appearance of the sky, it was agreed to keep up stream towards the lock. But before they reached it the first great drops of rain were splashing into the water about them. The lock-keeper made them welcome. He and Catterson were old acquaintances. Having set out for them, and dusted down three Windsor chairs, he went to spread a tarpaulin over the canoe.

The darkness of the little room grew deeper every instant. Then came an illuminating flash followed by a shattering thunder-peal. The ear was filled with the impetuous downrush of the rain.

"There! Why wouldn't you let me bring Gladys?" cried Nettie. "Poor little soul, she's so terrified of thunder, she'll scream herself into fits."

"She's right enough with Annie," said Catterson, somewhat too confidently.

Nettie replied that Annie was a perfect fool, more afraid of a storm than the child herself. "Jack, you'll have to go back and comfort her. Jack, you *must* go!"

"My dear, in this rain!" he expostulated. "How can you want me to do anything so mad?"

But Nettie had worked herself up into a paroxysm of maternal solicitude, of anguish of mind. West asked himself if it were entirely genuine, or partly a means of punishing Catterson for his self-assertion a while ago.

"Since you're so afraid of a little rain," she concluded contemptuously, "I'll go myself. I'm not going to let the child die in hysterics."

She made a movement as though to leave the house. Catterson drew her back, and turning up the collar of his coat, went out. But before the canoe was fairly launched, West knew he must be wet to the skin. He stood and watched him paddling down against the closely serried, glit-

tering lances of the rain, until lost in a haze of
watery grey.

Then, for his life, he could not refrain from
speaking. "I think it's very unwise for Jack to
get wet like that. It's not as though he were
particularly strong. He comes of a delicate,
short-lived family, as you probably know?"

But Nettie only stared silently before her as
though she had not heard.

And there, in silence, they remained for another
twenty minutes, while the rain flooded earth and
river, and the thunder rumbled to and fro about
the sky.

Nettie maintained an absolute silence, and West,
leaning against the window-frame, beguiled the
time in studying her with fleeting, inoffensive
glances. He again noted the ugliness of her
hands, to which, as they lay folded in her lap,
the flashing of a half-hoop of fine diamonds,
now worn above the wedding-ring, carried his
attention. But when he raised his eyes to her
small, pale face, he decided she was prettier than
she used to be, more strikingly pretty at first
sight. She had learned, perhaps, to bring out her
better points. He thought she dressed her hair
more becomingly ; three years steady application
of curling irons had at last induced it to lie in
softer curls. Five years of married life had in no
wise dimmed the transparency of her skin. Not

a line recorded an emotion whether of pleasure
or of pain. If she had lived through any psychic
experiences, they had not left the faintest trace
behind. And it was partly the immobility of
countenance by which this smoothness of surface
was maintained, which led West again to qualify
his favourable verdict, just as he had done in the
early moments of his acquaintance with her.

He began to think that the predominant note in
her character was coldness, heartlessness even.
He remembered, not so long ago, hearing her relate
as though it were a good story, how meeting old
Mrs. Baker one day in Kingston Market, she had
passed her by with an unrecognising stare. Yet the
old woman had been devoted to Nettie, as she herself used to boast ; a certain feeling of gratitude, of
kindliness might have been looked for in return.

But there must have been others, West told himself, to whom she owed a greater debt—the relations, or friends, who had brought her up, who had
clothed her and fed her until the day she had met
with Catterson. She never referred to these others,
she never let slip the smallest allusion to her early
life ; she held her secrets with a tenacity which
was really uncommon ; but it was evident that
she had turned her back on all who had ever be-
friended her with the same cold ease she had
shown to Mrs. Baker.

She was fond, apparently, of her little girl, but

this particular affection was no contradiction to her general want of it ; for she saw in the child a réduplication of herself. Gladys was the image of her mother, just as the little boy was Catterson over again ; very nervous, sensitive, and eager for love and approval.

West mused over the curious want of sympathy Nettie had always displayed for the boy. It amounted almost to dislike. He had never been able to win her good word from the day of his birth, and his natural timidity was greatly augmented by her severe treatment. West was inclined to believe the reason to be a sort of jealousy for Gladys; that she resented the fact that Cyril was legitimate, and would inherit under his grandfather's will, while the little girl, the first born, the preferred child, could not.

Catterson had never alluded to the subject, but for all that, West knew that he was profoundly hurt by the difference Nettie made between the children. If he himself made any in his heart— and West said it would be only natural if he loved Cyril most, who adored his father and impulsively showed it, rather than Gladys who always coldly repulsed his overtures of affection—at least in his conduct towards them he never let it appear. He even seemed to overlook Cyril a little, having learned by experience probably, what were the consequences of paying him too much attention.

Cyril was always left at home, while Gladys accompanied her parents everywhere.

Studying Nettie's physiognomy, tracing the lines of the mouth, the slightly backward drawn nostrils, the hard insensitive hands, West found himself rejoicing he did not stand in his poor little godson's shoes.

The storm was over, the sun was out again, and Nettie rising, suggested they should go. They crossed over the top of the lock-gates, picked their way between the puddles of the towing-path, and so back over Sonning Bridge to the hotel.

Catterson was in his room changing his wet clothes, and Nettie went up to him. West found Gladys sitting in the verandah beside her nurse, tranquilly playing with a doll.

"Well, babe," said he, in friendly tones, "were you very much frightened by the thunder and lightning, just now?"

But she did not answer, she merely fixed her limpid eyes on his, thrusting him back with their coldly negative stare. Then, ostentatiously, she re-absorbed herself in her game.

The next morning kept Catterson in bed with a bad cold, and West sooner than pass the day in the vicinity of Nettie, persuaded the nephew to abandon the aunt and the dinner, and both men into the extraordinary inconsistency of pushing on to Streatley.

III

ONE black morning in December, West remembered, for no reason at all, that it was the birthday of Cyril his godson. Cyril to-day entered on his fifth year, and West found himself making the usual "damned silly reflections" on the flight of time. Dismissing these as stale and unprofitable, he began to wonder what present he could take the boy. He tried to remember what he himself had liked at the age of four, but he could recall nothing of that antediluvian period. He thought of a book, a paint-box, a white fur rabbit, but the delights of painting and reading were surely beyond Cyril's years, while the Bunny was perhaps too infantile. Finally, he set his face westward, trusting to find inspiration in the windows of the shops he passed. The heavenly smell of chocolate which greeted him at Buszard's made him decide on a big packet of bon-bons. He knew from previous existence with the Catterson children, that chocolates were sure to be appreciated.

The Cimmerian morning had dragged its course

through brown, orange, and yellow hours, to an afternoon of misty grey. But West nevertheless felt inclined for walking. As he crossed the park diagonally from the Marble Arch to Queen's Gate, his thoughts outran his steps, and were already with the Cattersons.

They had moved again, and now lived in South Kensington. Nettie had become very intimate with a certain Mrs. Reade, whose acquaintance she owed to a week spent in the same hotel. The two young women had struck up an effusive friendship, based on a similarity of taste in dress and amusement, Mrs. Reade supplying the model for Nettie's faithful imitation. She copied her new friend's manners, she adopted her opinions and ideas. Mrs. Reade had declared it was impossible to live so far out of town as Surbiton. The Cattersons therefore disposed of the lease of their house, and took one close to Mrs. Reade's in Astwood Place.

Catterson had left his pretty suburban garden with the more reluctance that he disliked the Reades, considered the husband common, the wife loud, vulgar, bad style. But he had told West at the time, that no price was too high to pay for the purchase of domestic peace.

He was peaceably inclined by nature, but of late, any nervous energy which might have been contentiously employed, was used up in fighting

E

off the various trifling ailments that continuously beset him. He was always taking cold ; now it was lumbago, now a touch of congestion, now a touch of pleurisy. He spent half his days at home in the doctor's hands. Nettie made his bad health the ostensible reason for quitting Surbiton. The damp air rising from the river didn't suit him.

Town suited her, as she expressed it, " down to the ground," and following in Mrs. Reade's wake, she became one of the immense crowd of smartly-gowned nobodies, who, always talking as if they were somebodies, throng fashionable shops, cycle in the Park, and subscribe to Kensington Town Hall dances. It was far away from the days when she lived in lodgings at Teddington, made her own clothes, and cooked her own dinner.

Now she kept four maids, whom she was constantly changing. West seldom found the door opened by the same girl thrice. Nettie was an exacting mistress, and had no indulgence for the class from which presumably she had sprung. Her servants were expected to show the perfection of angels, the capacity for the work of machines, and the servility of slaves. And she was always detecting imperfections, laziness, or covert impertinence of manner or speech. Every six weeks or so there was a domestic crisis, and Mary or Jane left in tears, and without a character.

West could generally guess from the expression

of Jane's or Mary's face how long she had been in Astwood Place. Disappointment, harassment, and sullen discontent were the stages through which each new comer passed before reaching the tearful catastrophe.

From the serene appearance of the young person who to-day let him in, West judged she was but recently arrived. "Mrs. Catterson was out," for which he was not sorry; but "the Master was at home," which he had expected, having heard in the City that Catterson had not been at his office for some days.

He found him huddled up over the drawing-room fire, spreading out his thin hands to the blaze. Half lost in the depths of the armchair, sitting with rounded shoulders and sunken head, he seemed rather some little shrunken sexagenarian than a man still under thirty.

Gladys, with a picture-book open on her knee, sat on a stool against the fender. She did not move as West came in, but raising her eyes considered him, as was her wont, with a steadfast neutrality.

Catterson, turning, jumped up to greet him with something of his old buoyancy of manner; but the change which a few weeks had made in his face gave West a fresh shock. Nor could he disguise this painful impression sufficiently quickly.

"You think I'm looking ill, eh?" asserted Catterson, but with an eagerness which pleaded for a denial.

West lied instantly and heartily, but Catterson was not taken in.

"You think it's all U P with me, I see," he said, returning to the chair, and his former attitude of dejection.

This was so exaggerated a statement of his thoughts that West tried absolute candour.

"I don't think you're looking very fit," he said ; " but what you want is change. This dark, damp, beastly weather plays the deuce with us all. You should run down to Brighton for a few days. A man was telling me only last night that Brighton all this week has been just a blaze of sunshine."

"Oh, Brighton!" Catterson repeated, hope-lessly, "I'm past that." With the finger-tip of one hand he kept probing and pressing the back of the other as it lay open upon his knee, search-ing for symptoms of the disease he most dreaded.

To change the channel of his thoughts, West turned to the little girl who still mutely envisaged him.

"Well, Gladys, have you forgotten, as usual, who I am?"

"No, I haven't . . . you're Mithter Wetht," she told him, the piping drawl now complicated by a lisp, due to the fact that she had lost all her front teeth.

"Where's Sonny?" he asked her. "I've got something for him," and he put the packet of sweets down on the table.

She reflected a moment as to who Sonny might be; then, "Thyril'th a naughty boy," she said. "He'th had a good . . . whipping . . . and hath been put to bed."

"Oh poor old chap!" West exclaimed rue-fully, "and on his birthday too. What has he done?"

But Gladys only repeated, "He'th a . . . very . . . naughty boy," in tones of dogmatic convic-tion. She seemed to detect the guest's sympathy with the culprit, and to resent it.

Voices and laughter were heard on the stairs. Nettie entered in her bonnet and furs, preceded by a big, overdressed woman, whom West easily identified as Mrs. Reade. They had been shop-ping, and both were laden with small, draper's parcels.

Nettie did not seem pleased to find the drawing-room occupied. She gave West a limp hand without looking at him, which was one of her exasperating habits when put out, and then she attacked her husband for keeping up so big a fire. The heat of the room was intolerable, she said; it was enough to make any one ill. She threw off her wraps with an exaggeration of relief, peevishly altered the position of a chair which West had pushed aside inadvertently, and began to move about the room, in the search, as he knew well, of some fresh grievance. Catterson followed her for a second or two with tragic eyes. Then he turned to the fire again. " To me it seems very cold," he murmured ; " I've not been warm all day."

Mrs. Reade declared he should take to "byking." That would warm him ; there was nothing in the world like it. " Indeed unless it maims you for life, it cures every evil that flesh is heir to."

" But I suppose the chances are in favour of the maiming ? " West asked her.

She laughed hilariously at this, and though she was certainly vulgar, as Catterson had complained, West could not help liking her. He always did like the women who laughed at his little jokes. Mrs. Catterson never laughed at them.

Nettie wondered why on earth Jack could not have had tea ready, pulled violently at the bell, and began to examine some patterns of silk she had brought home with her, for the selection of an evening gown. Her lap was presently filled with little, oblong pieces of black and coloured brocades.

" The green is exquisite, isn't it, Mimi ? " she appealed to her friend, " but do you think it would suit me ? Wouldn't it make me look too pale ?

The heliotrope is lovely too, but then I had a gown last year almost that very shade. People would say I had only had it cleaned or turned. Perhaps, after all, I had better have black ? I've not had a black frock for a long time, and it's always so smart-looking, isn't it ? "

Mrs. Reade thought that in Nettie's place she should choose the green, and have it made up with myrtle velvet and cream guipure. An animated discussion of dressmaking details began, during which the men sat, perforce, silent.

Gladys, meanwhile, had come over to the table on which the chocolates lay, and now stood industriously picking open the paper.

Catterson presently caught sight of this.

" Gladys ! " he exclaimed, with the sharp irritability of ill-health.

She had just popped a fat bon-bon into her mouth, and she remained petrified for a moment by so unaccustomed a thing as a rebuke. Then for convenience sake, she took the sweet out again in her thumb and finger, and burst into sobs of anger and surprise.

Nettie was equally surprised and angry. " What are you thinking of, Jack, frightening the poor child by shouting at her like that ? "

" But did you see what she was doing, my dear, meddling with West's property ? "

" Mr. West shouldn't leave his sweets about on

the table if he doesn't want the child to have them. Naturally, she thought they were for her."

"Not at all. She knew they were for Cyril. She heard West say so."

"After Cyril's behaviour to me this morning I certainly shall not allow him to have them. And I don't approve of sweets anyway. It ruins the children's teeth. I wish Mr. West wouldn't bring them so often."

This was sufficiently ungracious, and West's answer was sufficiently foolish; "Perhaps you wish I wouldn't bring myself so often either?" said he.

"I've no doubt we could manage to get on just as well without you," she retorted, and there were worlds of insult concentrated in the tone.

The only effectual answer would have been immediate departure, but consideration for Catterson held West hesitant. It is always because of their affection for the husband that the wife finds it so particularly easy, and perhaps so agreeable, to insult his friends. She offers them their choice between perpetual banishment and chunks of humble-pie.

Catterson put an end to the situation himself.

"Let's get away out of this, West," he said, with flushed cheeks and shaking voice, "come down to my study."

Here, the change of atmosphere brought on a

fit of coughing, to which West listened with a
serrement de cœur. In his mind's eye he saw
Catterson again, vividly, as he had been a few
years back; very gay and light-hearted, full of
pranks and tricks. Always restless, always talking,
always in tip-top spirits; when he fell in love,
finding expression for the emotion in the whistling
and singing of appropriate love-ditties, the music-
hall love-ditties of the day.

The foolish refrain of one of these recurred to
West, ding-dong, pertinaciously at his ear:

> " They know me well at the County Bank,
> Cash is better than fame or rank,
> Then hey go lucky ! I'll marry me ducky,
> The Belle ci the Rose and Crown."

And now Catterson, with pinched features,
sunken eyes, and contracted chest, sat there
pouring out a flood of bitterness against himself,
life, and the gods for the granting of his prayer.

" You remember Nettie before I married her ?
Did she not appear the gentlest, the sweetest, the
most docile girl in the world? Who would ever
have imagined she could have learned to bully her
husband and insult his friends ?

" But the moment her position was assured she
changed; changed completely. Why, look here,
West, the very day we were married—you remember we went down to Brighton, and were

married there—as we walked back along the
King's Road, she stopped me before a shop and
said, 'You can just come in here and buy me
some furs. Now I'm your wife you needn't
suppose I'm going through another winter in my
wretched little old coat of last year.' It was her
tone; the implication of what she had had to
endure at my hands, before she had the right to
command me. It was the first lifting of the veil
on her true character.

"Perhaps if I had never married her — who
knows? Women require to be kept under, to be
afraid of you, to live in a condition of insecurity;
to know that their good fortune is dependent on
their good conduct.

"I did the right thing? Yes . . . but we are
told, be not righteous overmuch ; and there are
some virtues which dig their own graves."

He spoke in a disconnected manner ; but his
domestic misery was the string which threaded
the different beads. Of West's interjected sympathy and well-meant efforts to turn his thoughts
he took no heed.

"'Marriage is the metamorphosis of women.'
Where did I read that lately? It's odd ; but
everything I now read relates to marriage. In
every book I take up I find an emphatic warning
against it. Why couldn't these have come in my
way sooner ? Why couldn't some one tell me?

Marriage is the metamorphosis of women — the Circe wand which changes back all these smiling, gentle, tractable, little girls into their true forms.

"Oh, but after all, you say ? . . . No, my wife does none of those things ; but she has made my life miserable, miserable . . . and that's enough for me. And if I were to try and explain how she does it, I daresay you would only laugh at me. For there's nothing tragic in the process. It's the thousand pin-pricks of daily life, the little opposi- tions, the little perversities, the faint sneers. At first you let them slip off again almost indifferently, but the slightest blow, repeated upon the same place a thousand times, draws blood at last.

"No, she doesn't care for me, and sometimes I almost think she hates the boy. Poor boy . . . it seems monstrous, incredible; but I've caught her looking at him with a hardness, a coldness . . ."

He sat silent, looking wistfully away into space. West traced the beginning of a pleasanter train of ideas in the relaxed corners of his mouth, in the brightening of his sunken eyes.

"He's the dearest little chap, West! And so clever! Do you know, I believe he'll have the most extraordinarily logical and mathematical mind. He has begun to meditate already over what seems to him the arbitrariness of names. He wanted to know the other day, for instance, how a table had come to be called a table, why it wasn't called a chair, or anything else you like. And this morning, when we were talking, he and I, over the present I had given him, he posed me with this problem: Supposing two horses harnessed to a cart, were galloping with it, just as fast as ever they could go, how much faster could ten horses gallop with it? Shows he thinks, eh? Not bad for a child of four?"

He began to forecast Cyril's career; he would put his name down at Harrow, because to Harrow he could get out to see him every week. He should have the advantages of Oxford or Cambridge, which Catterson had not had. He should enter one of the liberal professions, the Bar for choice.

And then his face clouded over again.

"But he shall never marry. He shall do anything else in life he pleases: but he shall never marry. For it's no matter how well a man may be born, it's no matter how fortunate he may be in life, if he's unfortunate in his marriage. And it seems to me, that one way or another, marriage spells ruin."

He was back again in the unhappy present, and West felt his heart wrung. Yet there was no help to be given, no consolation possible. The one door of deliverance which stood open, was the one door which Catterson could not face, although his reluctant feet drew nearer to it every day.

But West had already observed that when life becomes impossible, when a man's strength is inadequate to the burdens imposed upon it, when the good he may yet accomplish is outweighed by the evils he may have to endure, then the door opens, the invisible hand beckons him through, and we know no further of his fate.

Though Catterson could not face it, and with an ominous spot burning on either cheek, tried to reabsorb himself again in plans for the future, West saw in it the only possible escape, and told himself it was better, even though it proved an eternal sleep, than what he daily had to endure.

The wife's cold heart, her little cruelties, her little meannesses, all her narrowness, all her emptiness of mind rose before him. What a hell upon earth to have to live in daily companionship with her, even if unrelated to her in any way! But for her husband she was the constant living reminder of his dead illusions. He could not look at her without seeing the poor, thin ghosts of his lost youth, of his shattered faith, hope, and happiness, gathered round her. Every indifference of hers, every neglect, must call up the memory of some warm protestation, of some dear attention in the past. And these were less hard to bear than the knowlege that those had never been genuine.

It is life as you anticipated it, brought still fresh

and palpitating into contrast with the bleak reality, which is so intolerably hard.

The contemplation of Catterson's position became so painful to West, that he felt he must get away even at the cost of brutality. He gave with warmth the asked-for assurance to come again soon, but he knew in his heart as he uttered it, that he would not soon find the courage to return.

In the hall he looked about him mechanically ; then let slip a hot and vigorous word on discovering he had left his hat up in the drawing-room, and must go back.

The tea-table now stood by Nettie's elbow. She insisted that he should take a cup of tea, pressing it on him as a sort of peace-offering, so that without actual rudeness he could not refuse. She was again gracious as far as she knew how to be. Possibly Mrs. Reade, who studied the suavities of life, had been remonstrating with her.

Gladys lay on the hearthrug, her face in her hands, her elbows planted on the open picture-book. The packet of sweets in a very knock-kneed and depleted condition stood beside her. She sucked a chocolate in her cheek, had kicked off her shoes, and drummed with her black-stockinged feet upon the floor.

West made a pretence of drinking his tea, but it was tepid, it was weak, and Nettie had put sugar into it without inquiring his tastes.

She and Mimi Reade were still discussing the patterns of the brocade.

"I do think the green quite heavenly, Mimi, in colour," she repeated, holding the scrap up at arm's length, so that the lamplight might slant over it; "and yet the black is a softer, richer silk, and would make up awfully well with jet trimmings, as you say. I don't know which I had better have."

The two women turned and re-turned the problem, considered it again in all its bearings. They appeared to have forgotten West, which was but natural, he had sat silent for so long. To himself, his brain seemed mesmerised by the vapidity of their talk, so that an imbecile point of interest grew up within it, as to which of the two silks, eventually, Nettie would choose.

Meanwhile the study door opened, and Catterson's cough, which carried such poignant suggestion to West, was heard again upon the stairs. It seemed to speak suggestively to Nettie too.

"After all," she said in her curious, drawling voice, "it would be more prudent, I suppose, to decide on the black."

AN ENGAGEMENT

AN ENGAGEMENT

WHEN Owen suddenly made up his mind again to tempt Fortune, and to invest the remnants of his capital in the purchase of Carrel's house and practice at Jacques-le-Port, he brought with him to the Island a letter of introduction to Mrs. Le Messurier, of Mon Désir.

But with the business of settling down upon his hands—and another distraction also—nearly six weeks went by before he remembered to call. Then, having inquired his way, he walked up to the house one mild, blue afternoon.

He found a spruce semi-detached villa, standing back from the road, with a finely sanded path running from the gate, right and left, up to the hall door. In the centre of the large oval flower-bed which the path thus enclosed, rose a tall and flourishing monkey-tree, with the comically ugly appearance to which Owen's eyes had grown familiarised since his coming to the Island. In front of nearly every villa is planted an araucania-tree.

Mon Désir was of two storeys, painted white, and had green wooden shutters turned back against the walls. Dazzlingly clean and very stiff lace curtains hung before the windows. Owen was favourably impressed, and, actuated by an unusual sentiment of diffidence, wondered who were the persons he should find within, and what sort of a reception awaited him.

The outer door of the house stood open, and the plate-glass panel of an inner door permitted him to see along a cool dark hall, tiled in black and white, into a sunny garden beyond. While he waited there, looking into the garden, a girl and boy passed across his range of vision, from one side to the other.

The girl was tall and slight, swung a gardening basket in one hand, and had the other arm laid round the shoulders of the boy, who was a whole head shorter than she. Although dowdily dressed in a frock of some dark material, although wearing a hideous brown mushroom hat, although she and her companion had scarcely come into sight before they had passed out of it again, nevertheless, Owen received in that fleeting moment the impression that she was pretty. And it left him absolutely indifferent.

Then a maid appeared from behind the stair-case, received his card and letter, and showed him into a small sitting-room on the left of the hall, a room so full of furniture, and at the same time so dark, that for a moment or two he was unable to find a seat. The light was not only materially obscured by the lace curtains he had noticed from the outside, but there were voluminous stuff curtains as well, and a green venetian blind had been let more than half-way down. Probably, earlier in the day the February sunshine had fallen upon the window, and consideration for the best parlour furniture is almost a religious cult among certain classes in the Island ; stray sunbeams are fought against with the same assiduity as stray moths. In all the neat villas which border the roads leading out from Jacques-le-Port, the best parlour is invariably a room of gloom, never used but on ceremonious occasions, or for the incarceration of such a chance and uninvited guest as was Owen to-day.

As his eyes accustomed themselves to the darkness he began to distinguish a multiplicity of Berlin wool cushions and bead-worked footstools, of rosewood *étagères* loaded with knick-knacks, and rosewood tables covered with photograph albums and gilt-bound books. He took up one or two of these and read the titles : " Law's Serious Call," " The Day and the Hour, or Notes on Prophecy," " Lectures on the Doctrine of the Holy Spirit." Such titles said nothing to him, and he put the volumes down again unopened. He began to study on the opposite wall a large coloured photograph of the Riviera ; the improbably blue sea, the incurving coastline, the verdure-clothed shore, dotted with innumerable white villas. But it interested him little more than the books had done, his acquaintance with foreign parts extending no farther than Paris.

He waited a few moments longer, and then two persons entered the room—a very old lady and the young girl he had caught a glimpse of in the garden. Seen now, without her hat, she was decidedly pretty, but Owen glanced past her to devote all his attention to Mrs. Le Messurier.

Giving him her hand, the old lady had said " How do you do ? " waiting until he had satisfied her as to the state of his health. Then she invited him to be seated, and introduced the young girl as " Agnes Allez, my granddaughter," only she pronounced the name " Orlay," which is the custom of the Island.

Miss Allez had said " How do you do ? " too, with a little air of prim gentility, which was the exact youthful counterpart of her grandmother's. After which she sat silent, with her hands lightly folded in her lap, and listened to the conversation.

Mrs. Le Messurier began with a few inquiries after the mutual acquaintance in England who had sent him to call upon her, and Owen replied suitably, while taking stock of her personality. She was dressed entirely in black, with a black silk apron over a black stuff gown, a black knitted shawl, a monumental cap of black lace and flowers and trembling bugles. The dress was fastened at the throat by a large gold brooch, framing a medallion of hair ingeniously tormented into the representation of a tombstone and a weeping willow-tree. An old-fashioned watch-chain of pale gold hung in two long festoons below her waist, and on her poor hand—a hand with time-stained, corrugated nails, with swollen, purple veins, with enlarged finger joints—a worn wedding-ring turned loosely.

Owen noted the signs of her age, of her infirmity, with half-conscious satisfaction; they promised him a patient before very long. And in the pleasant evidences of means all about him, he foresaw how satisfactorily he might adjust his sliding scale of charges.

She was speaking to him of his prospects in the Island, saying, with a melancholy motion of the head : " Ah, there, but for sure, you will have some trouble to work up Carrel's practice again. He have let it go all to pieces. An' such a good practice as it was in old Doctor Bragé's time. But you know the reason ? "

Owen knew the reason well. His predecessor had been steadily drinking himself to death for the last ten years, and his practice was as dilapidated as were his house, his dog-cart, his reputation. It was just on account of their dilapidations that Owen had bought these articles cheap ; while Carrel's reputation was of as little account to him as it was to Carrel himself, although it seemed likely, in spite of everything, to hang together longer than its owner would have any use for it.

"Well, I must try to work up Bragé's business again," said Owen self-confidently. With nervous tobacco-stained fingers he twisted and pointed one end of his black moustache, and became aware that the young girl was watching him covertly.

"There don't seem to be too many of us doctors here," he went on, "and from all I hear Lelever is very much behind the times. There ought to be a good opening, I should think, for a little new life, eh ?   A little new blood ?"

His voice touched an anxious note. The necessity of beginning to earn something pressed upon him. But Mrs. Le Messurier's reply was not reassuring.

"Ah, my good ! Doctor Lelever is, maybe, old-fashioned—I don't know nothing about that—but he is very much thought of. He is very safe, and he has attended us all. My poor boy John, who died of the consumption in '67; and my daughter, Agnes's mother, whom we lost when Freddy was born ; and my dear husband "—her knotted fingers went up to fondle mechanically the glazed tomb and willow-tree—"and poor Thomas Allez, my son-in-law, who went in '85."

Her dates came with all the readiness of constant reference.   She entered into details of the various complaints, the various remedies, the reasons they had failed.

Owen's face wore that smooth mask of sympathetic attention with which the profession equips every medical man, but he was embittered by the praises of Le Lièvre, and drawing the two ends of his moustache into his mouth he chewed them vexedly.

His discontented glance fell upon the young girl.   A sudden pink overflowed her cheeks.   He pointed his moustache again, smiled a little, and let his dark eyes fix hers with an amused complacency.   He saw he had made an impression.   She blushed a warmer rose, and looked away.

He wondered whether she talked the same broken English her grandmother did.   He hoped not ; but the four words she had as yet uttered left him in doubt.

Mrs. Le Messurier could not pronounce the "th."   She had said just now, speaking of Le Lièvre, "I don't know noddin' 'bout dat, but he is very much tought of."   And she laid stress on the unimportant words ; she accented the wrong syllables.   Owen felt it would be a pity if so kissable a mouth as Agnes Allez's were to maltreat the words it let slip in the same fashion.

He undertook to make her speak. The old lady had reached the catalogue of " Freddy's " infantile disorders, and as she coupled his name with no prefatory adjective of affection or commiseration, Owen concluded that he, at least, was still among the living, was probably the boy he had seen.

He turned to the young girl : " Then that was your brother you were with just now in the garden, I suppose ? "

She told him " Yes," and in reply to a further question, " Yes, he is only fifteen, and I shall be eighteen in May."

She spoke always with that little primness he had noticed in her reception of him, but her pronunciation was correct, was charming.

It occurred to him that the sunny February garden, and the companionship of the girl, would be an agreeable exchange for the starched and darkened atmosphere of the parlour and Mrs. Le Messurier's lugubrious reminiscences. He drew the conversation once and once again garden-wards, but without success.

To be guilty of anything so informal as to invite a stranger to step into the garden on his first visit was not to be thought of. The unconventional, the unexpected, are errors which the Islanders carefully eschew. Mrs. Le Messurier merely said :

"Yes, you must come up and drink tea with us one day next week, will you not, and the children will be very pleased to show you the garden then. What day shall it be ?"

The evening meal was at that moment ready laid out in the next room, and Owen, who had a long walk before him, would have been only too glad of an invitation to share it ; but it is not customary in the Islands to ask even a friend to take a cup of tea, unless the day and the hour have been settled at least a week in advance.

When Owen got back to his house in the Contrée Mansel, he found Carrel sitting over the fire in the dining-room, in a more than usually shaky condition. Carrel was always cold, and pleaded for the boon of a fire upon the warmest days. He paid Owen a pound a week for the privilege of boarding in the house where he had once been master, and spent the remainder of a small annuity on spirits. Owen made no effort to check him, not considering it worth his while. He saw that before long his room would be preferable to his company. However, for the present, he had his uses, he knew the Islands well, and when Owen chose to ask information from him, he could always give it.

He mentioned therefore where he had been, and inquired carelessly whether the old woman was worth money. Carrel, although very fuddled,

was still instructive. Oh yes, she had money sure
enough ; was a regular old Island woman, with
her head screwed on the right way about. But
Carrel doubted whether Owen would ever see the
colour of it. " Lelever's got the key of the situation there, my boy, and if he don't go off the
hooks before she does, he'll hold it till her death.
Unless, indeed, you can get round the soft side
of the granddaughter, little Agnes, hey ? Little
Agnes Allez. Good Lord, what a smashing fine
girl her mother was five-and-twenty years ago,
before she married that fool Tom Allez. He was
her cousin, too, and they were both the children
of first cousins. No wonder the boy's a natural.
Did ye see him, also ? "

Owen meditated ; then, referring to the grandmother, asked what she was worth. Carrel thought
she would cut up for ten thousand pounds.

" Which, laid out in good sound *rentes*, would
bring in £500 a year, and you would have the
house, and a nice little wife into the bargain.
And a family doctor is bound to marry, my boy,
hey ? Which reminds me to tell you," concluded
Carrel, with a spirituous laugh, " that your scarlet
devil of a Margot was here while you were out,
inquiring after you. I wonder what she'll do
when she hears you are making eyes at the little
Allez girl, hey ? "

" She may do as she damn pleases," said Owen,

equably; "do you imagine I'm in any way bound to a trull like that?"

But all the same he was sorry to hear that the red-haired witch had been round and that he had missed her. He had not seen her now for over a week.

⁂

An Island tea is a square, sit-down meal eaten in the living-room with much solemnity. It is taken at half-past five, and is the last meal of the day; you are offered nothing after it but a glass of home-made wine and a biscuit. It consists entirely of sweets; jams, cakes, and various *gôches* —*gôches à pommes, gôches à groseilles, gôches à beurre*. Sugar and milk are put liberally into every cup; and such hyper-inquisitiveness as a desire to know whether you take one or neither never occurs to the well-regulated Island mind. When you have eaten all you are able, you are urgently pressed to take a little more. It is considered good manners to do so.

When on the appointed day Owen found himself again at Mon Désir, he looked at Agnes Allez for the first time with a genuine interest. The ten thousand pounds mentioned by Carrel had stuck fast in the younger man's mind.

The girl sat at the tea-tray, and her grandmother faced her. The guest was at one side of the table, and the boy Frederic Allez on the other. Owen observed in him the same soft eyes, the same regular, well-proportioned features as his sister's. But his mouth would not stay shut, his fingers were never at rest, he laughed foolishly when he encountered Owen's gaze.

"I love dogs, they are so faithful," he told the visitor suddenly, à propos of nothing.

Owen assented.

His grandmother and sister did not pay him much attention, but a maid waited on him as though he were a child of six, passed him his tea, and placed wedges of cake and gôche upon his plate.

Mrs. Le Messurier ate little, folded her decrepit hands on the edge of the table, and looked on.

"I sometimes can't remember," she said, "that a whole generation has been taken away from me. When I look at Agnes and Freddy I could think it was the other Agnes and my boy John, who used to sit just so with me forty years ago. But we lived down in town then. Ah, but it is a pitée, a pitée, that they should have been taken, and a poor useless old woman like me left behind!"

Owen was infinitely bored by her regrets. He had no natural sympathy or patience with the old. He gave an audible sigh of relief when, tea over, it was proposed that Agnes should show him the garden. Small and well-kept, its paths were soon

explored ; but at the end was a little observatory
reached by a dozen wooden steps. A red-
cushioned bench ran round the interior, and the
front of the construction, of glass and three-sided,
gave an admirable view over immense skies and
an island-strewn sea.

"It's beautiful, is it not ? " said Agnes, with a
gentle pride in its beauty. "To me it seems quite
as beautiful as the Riviera. Not that I've ever been
there, of course, but gran'ma took poor Uncle John
there the last year of his life, and we have a picture
of it hanging in the drawing-room."

She named to Owen the different islands.
"That one is St. Maclou, and further on is the
Ile des Marchants. Over there to the left is the
Petite Ste. Marguerite. We can't often see the
Grande Ste. Marguerite without the glasses, but
Freddy will go and get them."

The boy who had given them his company the
whole time, punctuating their phrases with his
foolish laugh, blundered off on this errand with
an expression of consequential glee. Owen and
the girl were left alone.

The vast expanse of sea below them still glittered
in the light of the afterglow, but the cloud-curtain
of evening was drawing over the eastern sky—a
dreamy, delicious cloud-curtain of a soft lilac
colour, opaque and yet transparent, permitting
scintillating hints of the blue day behind to pierce

through.   And across its surface floated filmy
wreaths of a fading rose-colour, while high above
the observatory trembled the first faintly-shining
star.

But Owen looked only at the young girl, and
she grew embarrassed beneath his gaze. He
knew it was on his account she wore that elabo-
rate, but hopelessly provincial, Sunday frock;
on his account, that before coming out she had
gone upstairs to fetch her Sunday hat, instead of
putting on the every-day one which hung in the
hall.   He knew it was for him that she was blush-
ing so warmly; that it was to give herself a
countenance she fingered her sleeve so nervously,
unhooking it at the wrist, trying to hook it again,
not succeeding, and persisting in the attempt,
while every instant tinged her cheeks with a livelier
rose.

He watched her a few seconds, smiling behind
his moustache, before he leaned over, took hold
of her hand, and fastened the sleeve for her.   He
was pleasantly stimulated by the tremor he felt
running through her when his fingers touched
her skin.

Then the boy burst open the door, handed his
sister the glasses, and flung himself down, with
his wearying laugh, on the cushion by her side.

" I love dogs," he said to Owen, just as he had
done at tea, "don't you ?   They are so faithful."

It appeared to be a stock phrase of his, beyond which he could not get.

.

During the next six weeks Owen was often at Mon Désir, and his visits to Agnes and his assignations with Margot afforded him agreeable alternative recreation from his work.

He had known for long, however, that Agnes was in love with him—he had for long made up his mind that she and her ten thousand pounds were desirable possessions—before he said any word to the girl herself. And then, as generally happens, the crisis came fortuitously, unpremeditatedly. They were out on the cliffs together. She had been showing him Berceau Bay, which lies below Mon Désir. They had stepped from a door in the garden into a green lane, and had followed it down, down through veils and mazes of April greenness, until it suddenly stopped with them on a grassy plateau overlooking the winged bay. At their feet the shadow of the hill behind them lay upon the water, but out beyond the shadow, the sea sparkled with jewel-like colour and brilliancy. When they had climbed the steep cliff path on the other side, they had stopped a moment to notice the gulls and cormorants perched on the rock-ledges beneath them, and all at once the decisive words had passed his lips, and the girl was looking up at him with soft brown eyes that overflowed with love, with tears, before he quite knew how it had come about. But after all, he was glad to have it settled, and to have the engagement sealed and confirmed that same night by Mrs. Le Messurier's tremulous, hesitating, not over-cordial sanction.

No, she was not over-cordial, the old skin-flint, he told himself as he went away, not so grateful as she should have been, but all the same, this disconcerting element in her attitude did not prevent him from boasting complacently of his good fortune to Carrel, the moment he got home.

Carrel happened to be comparatively sober, and his mood then was invariably a fleering one. For his heart fed on a furious hatred and envy of Owen. He envied him his twenty-eight years, he envied his sobriety, his strength of character. He hated his ill-breeding, his cock-sureness, his low ambitions. And though he had been glad enough when Owen had purchased the house and practice, he chose now to consider him an interloper who had ousted him from his proper place. He therefore at once planted a knife in Owen's vanity, and gave him some information he had previously held back.

"So you are going to marry little Agnes Allez ? Well, you might do worse. The old lady is bound to leave her a nice little nest egg, but I expect she'll tie it up pretty tight too. She and the old man didn't spend forty years of their lives in the drapery business, saving ha'pence, for the first vagrant Englishman who comes along to have the squandering of."

" What's that ?" said Owen sharply, unable to conceal his disgust.

Carrel turned the knife round with dexterous fingers. " You didn't suppose she was one of the Le Mesuriers of Rozaine, did you ? Pooh ! She kept the shop in the High Street which Roget has now, and that's where the money comes from."

Owen, the son of a third-rate London attorney, naturally recoiled from the prospect of an alliance with retail trade. But perhaps Allez, the father, had been a gentleman ?

Carrel quenched this hope at once.

" Tom Allez was son of a man who kept a fruit-stall in the Arcade. He couldn't afford to stock himself, but sold for the growers on commission. However, towards the end of his life, he began to grow tomatoes himself out Cottu way, and was doing very well when he died, and Tom, who was always an ass, brought everything to rack and ruin. But he was already married to Agnes Le Messurier, so the old people took the pair of 'em home, to live with them. And Tom never did anything for the rest of his life but develop Bright's disease, which carried him off when he

was forty-one.   The boy is an imbecile, as you see.
And, by the bye, in counting your eggs, he must
be reckoned with.   Half the money will go to him,
you may be sure.   I doubt whether little Agnes
will get more than two hundred a year after all."

For twenty-four hours Owen meditated on this
news, weighing in the balance his social ambitions
against a possible five thousand pounds.

Then he came to Carrel again.   " Look here,"
he said, " you understand these damned little
Islands better than I do.   Would it really make
any difference in my career to contract such a
marriage ? "

" It would only keep you out of the society of
the precious Sixties you're so anxious to cultivate,
for the rest of your life," chuckled Carrel ; " it
would only be remembered against you to the
sixth generation.   At present, as an outsider, a
stranger, you are in neither camp, but once you
marry a Le Messurier with two s's, you place
yourself among the Forties for ever."

From this date onwards, Owen's speculations
were given to the problem of how he could easiest
get loose from his engagement.

•
• •

Agnes Allez stood in her bedroom, tortured by
apprehension and suspense.   She asked herself
what could be going on in the best parlour below

where Owen was closeted with her grandmother, and she forbidden to join them. Her grandmother had written to Owen, asking him to call upon her, and had said to the girl, before he came, "Now, perhaps I shall send for you, but until I do, remain in your room."

Already, half an hour, three quarters of an hour, had gone by, and the longed-for summons did not reach her; her keen ears still detected the murmurous rumble of voices downstairs. Then, of a sudden, they ceased : she heard the glass door of the hall shut to, and, from outside, firm steps grind down the gravel. She ran to the open window, and through the slots of the shutters saw Owen's tall figure pass down the path and out of the gate. He never once turned his head, but, taking the road to Jacques-le Port, was lost to view behind its trees. Then came her grandmother calling to her from the hall, and she went down.

Mrs. Le Messurier told her, with kindness indeed, but with the melancholy satisfaction also, which the very old find in evil tidings, that her engagement with Dr. Owen must be considered at an end. She had never completely approved of him, but lately she had heard stories, which, if true, could only merit the severest condemnation. She had given him the opportunity of demonstrating their falsehood. He had failed to do so to her satisfaction, and thereupon she had told him, as she now told Agnes, that the engagement between them was at an end.

The girl's first feeling was one of burning indignation against the persons who had dared to slander the man she loved. She knew little of what had been said, she understood less, but she was sure, she was convinced, before hearing anything, that it was all untrue.

"Pedvinn talks of bringing an action against Thoumes and his wife," Mrs. Le Messurier told her, "for misappropriating poor Louis Rennuf's property."

"But not against Jack, I suppose, because he could not keep the poor old man alive!" Agnes cried, with flaming cheeks. Renouf was a patient of Owen's, who had died about three weeks before.

"The girl Margot has been seen going in and out of the surgery ever since your engagement, child."

"And suppose she has," cried Agnes, astonished, "what harm is there in that ?"

But when her first anger had cooled down she awoke to a sense of her own misery, to a sense of the cruelty of her fate. She had not been engaged three months, and already the beautiful dream which had come into her life was shattered at a touch. Until the unforgettable moment when Owen had first called at Mon Désir, she had led such dull, such monotonous days ; not unhappy ones, simply because she had known no happier ones to gauge them by. She had often smiled since to remember that she had been used to find excitement in a summer picnic with the de Gruchy girls at Rocquaine, in a winter lecture with magic-lantern illustrations at the Town Library.

In those days she had known of love in much the same vague unrealising way that she had known of the Desert of Sahara; although she had touched the fringe of courtship when young Mallienne, the builder's son, had offered her peppermints during evening chapel one Sunday last December. When she met him after that she used to smile and blush.

She, of course, had always supposed that she should some day marry. Everybody did. Last summer her friend Caroline de Gruchy had married Mr. Geraud, pharmacien at St. Héliers; but he was bald, forty years of age, and not at all handsome, and although Agnes had been one of the bridesmaids, the affair had left her cold and unmoved.

But with Owen's first visit she had awoke suddenly to the knowledge of love, and this wonderful fact, this stupendous miracle rather, had changed for her the whole world. It was as though she were endowed with a new sense; she saw meaning and beauty everywhere; her perceptions acquired clearness at the same time that

her eyes grew deeper, more intense, that her cheek
took on a lovelier colour, her mouth a sweeter, a
more engaging smile.

Every hour, every moment, that she had spent
in Owen's company was indelibly engraved on
her memory. She could call up each particular
occasion at will. She had learned his portrait off
by heart at that first visit, she had done nothing
but add graces to it ever since. She thought him
the most handsome, the most distinguished-looking
man she had ever seen. She admired his black
hair, his dark eyes, his sallow skin.   She admired
the way he held himself, the way he dressed,
although she had observed on the same occasion
that the stiff edges of his cuffs were frayed, although
she had seen, as she watched him away from the
door, that his boot-heels were trodden down on
the outside. But in spite of his shabby clothes,
he looked a thousand times the superior of young
Mallienne, of any of the young men she knew, in
their best Sunday broadcloth.

And this was before she had formulated, even
to herself, her feelings for him ; long before that
ecstatic, that magical moment, when he had taken
her into his arms, had kissed her, had kissed her
mouth, had said, " Well, little one, do you know
I am very fond of you, and I fancy you don't
altogether dislike me, eh ? "

That had happened on a Sunday afternoon,

April 28th ; a date she could never forget. They
were out upon the *côte ;* Freddy was nominally
with them, but in point of fact had wandered away
to gather the wild hyacinths which just then car-
peted the ground with blue. He kept bringing her
bunches of these to take care of ; she could feel
again the thick, pale-green, shiny stems grasped
in her hand. She and Owen climbed the steep
path which winds up from the bay to the brow of
the cliff ; her dress brushed against the encroaching
gorse and bracken, and her eyes followed a couple
of white butterflies gyrating on ahead ; when she
looked down from the height on which she stood,
she saw the smooth sea below her, paving, as with
a green translucent marble, every inlet, every
crevice of the bay.

Then the path had bent outwards to skirt a
great boulder of granite, and there, right under
the shelter of the rock, was a circular clearing,
a resting-place, spread with the sweet, short cliff-
grass, where a broad ledge of the stone offered a
natural seat.

It was here that he had kissed her, and the
flowers had fallen in a blue confusion at her feet,
and, " Oh, I love you so," she had whispered, and
he had laughed, and said, " Yes, child, I could see
that from the very first."

Then they had sat down, he with his arm round
her waist. " Well, I must call you Agnes now,

I suppose," he had said; and she had timidly asked him his name, and he had told her, John Ashford Owen, but that his friends commonly called him Jack. " Then I may call you Jack, too, because I am going to be your best friend of all," she had answered, and on this Freddy had come up and broken into loud lamentation over the scattered flowers. To appease him they had both knelt down in the grass and helped him gather them up.

Jack had kissed her many times since, but never perhaps in quite the same way. At least, she had never experienced since quite the same sweet tremulous emotion. And yet she loved him more devotedly every day. Every day her affection sent out fresh delicate tendrils which rooted themselves inextricably in him.

And now these were to be rudely torn up; at a word all her joy, all her heaven was to come to an end. It was too cruel. And for what reason ? Because wicked, envious people invented calumnies concerning him. It was too monstrous.

She passed a miserable night, but with the morning plucked up faint heart again. For it was impossible her engagement should really for ever be at an end. With a little time, a little patience, things must come right. Her sufferings were now all for Jack. How wounded, how outraged he must have felt, never even to

have looked back when on Saturday he had left
the house.

Oh, she must write to him, must tell him to
have courage, not to give her up, and all would
yet be well.

In the warm, silent solitude of her shuttered
bedroom she wrote her first love-letter, an adorable,
naïve, rambling letter; and waited in fluttering
expectation during three interminable days for his
reply. When it came, she had to read it twice
over before she understood it. Correctly expressed, formal, in his rather illegible hand
sprawling over two sides of the paper, Owen
wrote that he had too much self-respect to wish
to force himself on a family where he was not
appreciated, and too high a sense of honour to
accept her well-meant proposal for a clandestine
engagement.

When understanding came, she broke into
floods of weeping; then dried her tears, and
sought excuses for his seeming coldness. She
found them in his pride; it was naturally up in
arms, after the rebuff it had received. If he had
addressed her merely as " My dear Agnes," that
was because he thought it probable Mrs. Le Messurier would see the letter; but he had signed
himself "Yours, nevertheless." This was intended
to show her he loved her still. Before evening,
the very cause of her morning's anguish was con-

verted into another proof of the nobility of her lover's mind.

By the end of twenty-four hours she had persuaded herself she ought to write to him again, to reproach him gently, tenderly, for his attitude towards her, to assure him of her unalterable constancy, to implore him, too, to be true. This letter was written on a Sunday, and she carried it to evening chapel with her, inside the bosom of her frock, both to sanctify it as it were, and to have the pleasure of feeling it against her heart as long as possible. Happy letter! by to-morrow morning it was to have the joy, the glory, of lying in *his* hand. Her grandmother never went to chapel a second time, and Freddy made no objection to passing round by the letter-box on the way home.

There was a day of long suspense, but when Agnes came down to breakfast on Tuesday morning, purposely earlier than the others, she found Owen's answer lying on her plate.

With her heart beating violently, she took it up, studied every line, every dot of the superscription, noticed that the stamp had been put on crookedly, that the flap of the envelope went down into a long point. She turned it over and over in her hand, filled with a sort of sweet terror as she speculated on its contents. But the fear that in a few moments she would no longer be alone came to determine her. She pulled it hastily open, tearing the envelope into great jags, and unfolded a sheet of note-paper which contained five lines. They began, " Dear Miss Allez," expressed polite regret that Mrs. Le Messurier's decided action in the matter made it impossible the writer should permit himself any longer the pleasure of corresponding with her, and were signed "Very truly yours, J. Ashford Owen."

The girl turned red, then white. Her hands trembled, her blood ran cold. She heard her grandmother and Freddy in the hall. To hide her emotion, she got up and walked over to the window. The August flowers in the garden seemed to look at her with crooked jeering eyes.

Jack had written her a horrible letter; she repeated this to herself over and over again during the day. He had no heart. She thought of all that had passed between them ; she called up, line by line, every word of her letter to him. Her cheeks burned with shame. She hated him, hated him. She would renounce him entirely, never think of him again. But even while she said it, she burst into tears, flung herself upon her bed, and kissed and passionately kissed the letter which had pierced her heart.

Therewith she began again the eternal rehabilitative process, in which every woman shows herself such an adept in relation to the man she loves.

Jack had not meant to be cruel, but he was quick-tempered; he resented the treatment he had received. Still smarting from a sense of injury, he would naturally be unjust towards every one, angry even with her. But, of course, he loved her all the same. He had loved her only a few weeks ago. One could not change so absolutely in so short a time. One could not love and not love as one puts on and off a coat. It was she who was wicked to doubt him, who was unreasonable not to make allowances, who was stupid not to read his real feelings beneath the disguising words.

But no sooner was her idol again set upon his altar, than doubt, suspicion, assailed her anew. And so the struggle continued between her longing to believe her lover perfect and the revolt of her reason, her dignity, against his conduct towards her. Yet with every victory love flowed stronger, resentment ebbed insensibly away.

* * *

The last traces of resentment vanished when one Saturday in town she met him suddenly face to face. She was passing the Town Library, and exactly as she passed, Owen came out, standing still, as he saw her, on the step.

Her pulses beat tumultuously, the colour ran to her cheeks.

"Oh, Jack," she cried, taking his hand, "how could you write to me so coldly, so cruelly? If you knew what I have suffered! And it was not my fault . . ."

From the first moment of seeing her, Owen had stood transfixed, silent. Now he pushed back the swing door, and held it wide.

"At least come in here," he said slowly; "don't let us have a scene in the street."

They stood together in a corner of the great, granite-flagged hall, which offered such cool, quiet contrast with the sunshine and turmoil outside.

"You don't care for me any more?" she asked, keen for the denial, which came indeed, but which to her supersensitiveness seemed to lack emphasis.

But his excuses were emphatic enough.

"It's no more my fault than it's yours," he told her; "it's your grandmother who won't have anything to say to me, the Lord knows why?"

He spoke interrogatively, and she flamed a deprecating crimson.

"I can't very well force my way into the house against her wishes, can I?" he went on.

"No; but, dearest Jack, you needn't be angry with me, and we can wait a little, and I know everything will come right. If only you will go on loving me. You do love me still?" she asked him, "I shall die if you don't!"

He smiled down upon her, twisting his moustache-end. A softer look came into his eyes.

" So the poor little girlie can't live without me ? " he said, and gently squeezed her arm. Her heart welled up with adoration and gratitude.

A stranger coming down the polished wooden staircase cast a sympathetic glance at this little Island love idyll.

But Owen looked at his watch.

" Oh, confound it ! Half-past twelve already, and I ought to be up at Rohais by now. I've an appointment there. I don't like to leave you, but——"

" Is it *very* important ? " she asked wistfully.

" It's a new patient."

" Oh, then in that case, of course you must go," she admitted, with ready abnegation of her pleasure where it clashed with his interests. " But when shall I see you again ? Ah, do let me see you."

" Oh, . . . well, . . . all right ! I'll stroll up to-morrow in the course of the afternoon, to Berceau Bay . . . but if I'm prevented, you'll be coming to market, next Saturday, I suppose, eh ? "

And he was gone.

Agnes sat down for a few moments to recover her composure. Her eyes rested on the red gold-fish swimming futilely round and round the glass bowl in the centre of the hall ; but at her ear was the joy-killing whisper that the appointment had been a fictitious one.

Nevertheless, she persuaded herself he would come next day. She spent three hours, hidden in the bracken, at a point whence she could overlook the whole bay. When he did not come, she deferred her hopes to the following Saturday, to be again disappointed. He was not to be seen. Neither in the Market Place, nor at the Library, nor yet in the Contrée Mansel; for she could not refrain from the poor pleasure of passing along the street in which he lived, of glancing shame-facedly at his house, of envying wildly the servant she saw for an instant at an upper window. She would have thought it a privilege to be allowed to clean his boots.

But when she found herself at home that evening she was seized by an access of silent despair. There seemed nothing on earth to do : nothing to live for.

Yet the buoyancy of youth is hard to extin-guish. Repeated blows are needed to beat it down, just as the tears shed at eighteen may be bitter indeed, but do not furrow the cheeks.

.

As the year brought round another spring, Agnes found that her spirits grew brighter with the days. She loved Jack more than ever. It

H

was impossible to be absolutely unhappy with such a love in her heart ; with the knowledge that she lived in the same Island with him ; that once a week at least she could walk through the streets he daily trod ; that any day she ran the chance of meeting him again, of speaking with some one who had just spoken with him.

Against dates on which she heard his name thus mentioned, she put a cross of red ink in the little calendar she carried in her purse. When she was having her new summer frock fitted, the dress-maker's three-year-old child ran into the room. Agnes, who was fond of children, said a kind word to him ; but the mother, kneeling on the floor with upstretched arms and a mouthful of pins, shook her head menacingly.

" Ah, Johnnie's a bad boy. He won't take his medicine. I'll have to tell Dr. Owen 'bout him."

" Does Dr. Owen attend him ?" Agnes asked, flutteringly ; and the woman explained Owen was doctor of the club to which her husband belonged.

" He's a very clever doctor," ventured Agnes, all covered with blushes. " Don't you think so ? "

" Ah, my good ! " said the other, as who should say, doctors are necessary evils, and there's not much to choose between them. " But he give Johnnie a fine new double piece last time he come, didn't he, Johnnie ? 'Tisn't the value I ever looks at," she explained to Agnes, "but the kind thought."

Agnes felt a glow of pride at the generosity, the
good-heartedness of her lover, and on going away
she pressed a whole British shilling into Johnnie's
treacly little paw. Against this day she placed
two crosses in her calendar, and the episode filled
her thoughts for a week, to be succeeded by a
still more precious one.

The annual picnic came round, provided by the
Chapel for its Sunday-school. Agnes, as one of
the teachers, went with the rest. They drove in
waggonnettes to Rocquaine, and the only point
of the day to which she looked forward with
pleasure, was the passing Owen's house on the
way back late at night. They went by a longer
way, but they always came down the Contrée
Mansel on the way home. She distinguished
from quite a distance *his* illuminated parlour
window ; but the white blind was drawn down ;
she was just going to be bitterly disappointed,
when a shadow, *his* shadow, passed across it. She
thrilled with excitement, with gratitude for her
great good luck, and answered young Mallienne,
who sat beside her, with strange irrelevancy.

For in spite of everything she could not realise
to herself that Owen did not love her ; her heart
refused to envisage it. Although he made no
effort to see her, although he gave no sign, she
clung to the belief that all would yet be well.
She leaned on Fate ; something would be sure to

happen . . . some day, when she was her own
mistress . . . She thought of him constantly, loved
him as tenderly as before.

•.•

The summer was extraordinarily fine. The heat
which had begun in March, lasted right through
to September ; in the middle of the day from July
onwards, it was almost unbearable. Agnes, one
Saturday, having been into town as usual, was
obliged to walk home laden with purchases, for
the omnibus filled up with waiting passengers
almost the moment it reached the Market Place.
But when, very warm and a little weary, she
reached Mon Désir, she found Frederic in one of
those states of nervous excitement from which he
periodically suffered. Mrs. Le Messurier had given
him a soothing draught, the last in the house.
It was essential to have more in case another were
required durng the night or the next day.

Agnes, pleased at the chance of a second journey into town, since it gave her a second chance
of meeting Owen, volunteered to go back for it.
Mrs. Le Messurier told her she looked done up
with the heat already, but that she might go when
she had had her dinner, and that she must take
the omnibus both ways.

It was half-past two when she reached town,
crossed over to Mauger's, and waited there while

the prescription was made up. She had then ten minutes on her hands before the three o'clock omnibus left for St. Gilles.

An old family friend, Mr. de Gruchy, stood in his shirt-sleeves on the threshold of his shop. Agnes stopped to speak to him, and to inquire after the girls. They were all away from home, and doing well. Their mother received cheerful letters every week. Agnes charged him with kind messages for them, and turned to go. He shook her hand heartily. " Well, good-bye, my dear," he said, in his comfortable, resonant voice, " my love to your grand'ma, and ask her when she's going to spend another day with us, eh ? "

Coming down the street were a lady and two gentlemen. The men were in tennis flannels, and carried racquets and balls. The girl wore a lilac and white frock, fashioned with a simplicity and *chic* that spoke of St. Héliers at least, if not of Paris.

Agnes recognised the youngest Miss d'Aldernois, her brother the Captain, just back from India, and between the two, Jack Owen. Jack was looking straight towards her.

The delighted blood sprang to her cheek, her eyes sparkled, her mouth smiled. She took a step forward, she half extended her hand . . . and he looked her full in the face without a sign of recognition and passed on.

Miss d'Aldernois' silk-lined skirt brushed with a light frou-frou against hers, as, with her pretty head held high, she chattered volubly with her pretty lisp. The Captain walked in the roadway.

Agnes stood and watched the three figures with their short, slanting shadows retire further and further down the sunny street.

"Come in and take something, my dear," she heard de Gruchy saying at her elbow; "a little drop of raspberry vinegar now, it will do you good. Or go up and have a chat with mother, eh? You will find her in the drawing-room. She would like to read you Lucy's last letter, I know. It's downright clever."

Agnes shook her head, stammered excuses in a voice that sounded strange in her own ears, and left him.

He had cut her dead; Jack, the man she worshipped. The only man who had ever taken her in his arms and kissed her; the only man by whom she ever wished to be kissed and held. In broad daylight, openly, before witnesses, he had cut her.

Mr. de Gruchy had seen what had happened; he had understood; he had pitied her.

An illumination came. Jack was ashamed of her. Because she had shaken hands with the old man, he was ashamed to recognise her before his new friends. She was connected with trade; a

child of trade ; and he was now received among
the Sixties.

A profound humiliation overpowered her,
sapped the rest of her strength. The glare of the
sun became suddenly intolerable . . . she longed
to be at home, to be in darkness.

She discovered that in her preoccupation she
had taken the wrong turning. She hurried back,
but the market clock showed seven minutes past
three. The omnibus must be already half-way
up Constitution Hill.

There was nothing to do but to walk, as she
had walked in the morning. She set out with
automatic movements, with a suffering endurance.

When you step away from the last bit of shadow
of the town, and, steeply climbing, reach the level
hill-top, you have before you a long unsheltered
stretch of road until you come to the trees of
St. Gilles. It is a white and dusty road with sun-
parched fields on either side ; and in July there
is a blazing sky above you, to your left a blazing
sea.

It seemed to Agnes that the sun was darting his
rays straight down into her brain, that the ground
was scorching the soles of her feet. But it did
not occur to her to open her umbrella.

The passing scarlet jacket of a soldier made her
close her eyes with pain. The whistle of a boy
behind her set all her nerves ajar.

Should she ever get home? . . . She dragged on with leaden feet and prayed persistently for darkness.

But when at last she lay upon her own bed in such darkness as closed shutters and drawn curtains can give, all she could say was, "Oh, the sun, the sun!" all she could do was to lift her hand indeterminately towards her head. And when, a few hours before the end, she lost the power of speech, still her hand wandered up every now and again automatically towards her head.

.

Mrs. Le Messurier sits alone with her grandson in the living-room of Mon Désir. He cuts out pictures from the illustrated papers, and she gazes tirelessly through dim and tearless eyes into the past. Bright crowds of long-dead men and women pass before her, and among them the two Agneses are never absent long. Then, all at once, as the boy, with his mirthless laugh, looks up to claim her attention, the vision is scattered into thin wreaths of smoke.

THE WEB OF MAYA

THE WEB OF MAYA

I

LE TAS is the name of the land lying at the southern extremity of the Isle of Saint Maclou. It would form a separate islet by itself, but that it is joined to the larger one by an isthmus, a wall of rock, of such dizzy height, of such sheer descent, that the narrow road on top gropes falteringly its perilous way from side to side.

The fishermen of Saint Maclou, who are also its farmers, its field-labourers, its coachmen, when driving a party of trippers over to Le Tas, get down at the beginning of the Coupée, as this strange isthmus is called, and, in their courteous broken English, invite their fares to get down too Then, holding the horse by the bridle, and walking backwards before him, the driver leads him over the Coupée, turning an anxious eye this side and the other, to see that the wheels keep within the meagre limits : for, a careless movement here

—a false step—and you would be precipitated down a clear three hundred feet to the sea below. But it is only an experienced fisherman who will take you over the Coupée at all. If a young man happens to be driving, he will send you into Le Tas on foot, while he smokes his cigar, as he waits for you in safety, at the Saint Maclou end.

Le Tas, as its name suggests, is just a mound or heap of rocks. Flung up there by the sea, ages ago, the same sea has already so undermined it, so under-tunnelled it, that with a few ages more it must crumble in, and sink again to the ocean bed from which it came.

There are very few houses on Saint Maclou; besides the Seigneurie, the Rectory, and the Belle Vue Hotel, perhaps only some forty homesteads and cottages. On Le Tas there are but five all told. You come upon four of these shortly after crossing the Coupée. Grouped together in a hollow which hides them from the road, they are still further hidden by the trees planted to shelter them from the great westerly gales. But, should you happen to make your way down to them, you would discover a homely and genial picture : little gardens ablaze with flowers, tethered cows munching the grass, fowls clucking, pigeons preening themselves and cooing, children playing on the thresholds, perhaps a woman, in the black sun-bonnet of the Islands, hanging her linen out to dry, between the gnarled apple-trees of the orchard on the right.

When you have left these cottages behind you, Le Tas grows wilder and more barren with every step you take. At first you walk through gorse and bracken ; patches of purple heather contrast with straggling patches of golden ragwort. But, further on, nothing grows from the thin layer of wind-carried soil, save a short grass, spread out like a mantle of worn green velvet, through which bare granite knees and elbows protrude at every point. You see no sign of life, but a goat or two browsing on the steep declivities, the rabbits scudding among the ferns, the rows of cormorants standing in dark sedateness on the rocks below. You hear nothing but the strange complaining cry of the sea-gull, as it floats above your head on wide-spreading motionless wings, and draws, as by an invisible string, a swift-flying shadow far behind it, over the sunny turf.

Here, at the very end of Le Tas, facing the sea, stands the fifth house, a low squalid cottage, or rather a row of cottages, built of wood, and tarred over, with a long, unbroken, shed-like roof of slate. It has no garden, no yard, nor any sort of enclosure, but stands set down barely there upon the grass, as a child sets down a toy house upon a table.

It was built to lodge the miners, when, forty

years since, great hopes were entertained of extracting silver from the granite of Le Tas. Shafts were sunk, a plant imported, a row of half-a-dozen one-roomed cottages run up on the summit of the rock. But the little silver that was found never paid the expenses of working. The mines were long ago abandoned, though the stone chimneys of their shafts still raise their heads among the bracken, and, whitewashed over, serve as extra landmarks to the boatmen out at sea.

The cottages had been long disused, or only intermittently inhabited, until, one day, Philip Le Mesurier, of Jersey, called upon the Seigneur, and offered to rent them for himself. It was just after Le Mesurier's six years of unhappy married life had come to an end. Mrs. Le Mesurier had, one night, without any warning, left Rozaine Manor, taking her little son with her, and she had absolutely refused to go back, or to live with her husband again. There had been a great scandal. The noise of it had spread through the Islands. It had even reached Saint Maclou. Women said that Le Mesurier had ill-used his wife shamefully, had beaten her before the servants, had habitually permitted himself the most disgusting language. He was known to have the Le Mesurier violent temper; he was suspected of having the Le Mesurier taste for drink. Lily Le Mesurier, on the other hand, was spoken of as the sweetest, the most long-suffering of God's creatures, a martyred angel, against whom, though she was young and pretty, no worse fault could be alleged than that she was "clever" and read "deep" books. A most devoted mother, it was only when she at last realised that she must not expose her child to the daily degradation of his father's example, that she had finally determined upon a step so inexpressibly painful to her feelings as a separation.

A few men shrugged their shoulders; said they should like to hear Le Mesurier's side of the story; but knew they would never hear it, as he was much too proud to stoop to self-excusings.

The Seigneur of Saint Maclou was among those whose sympathies went with Le Mesurier. They had a club acquaintanceship in Jersey. He welcomed him to Saint Maclou; converted the "Barracks," as the cottages on Le Tas were called, into a single house, more or less convenient; and hoped that during the short time Le Mesurier would probably remain on the island, he would come often to the Seigneurie.

The young man thanked him, sent over a little furniture, came himself, with his guns, his fishing tackle, his paint-box and canvases, and took up his residence in the Barracks. But he went very seldom to the Seigneurie, where he ran the risk of meeting visitors from Jersey; and when this had

happened on two occasions, he went there no more.
And he stayed on at Le Tas long after the reason
he had given for his presence—that he had come
for a holiday, to shoot, to fish, to sketch—had
ceased to find credence. He stayed on through the
autumn, through the winter, through the spring;
he neither fished, nor shot, nor painted; he held no
intercourse with anyone; he lived entirely alone.
The only person with whom he ever exchanged a
word was Monsieur Chauchat, the French pastor.
Sometimes, in the evening, Le Mesurier would
walk over to Saint Maclou, and smoke a pipe at
the Rectory; sometimes when the weather was
tempting, the old clergyman, who liked him and
pitied him, would come up in the afternoon to
pay a visit to the Barracks; but these meetings
between them were rare, and, as Le Mesurier
grew more moody, and Chauchat more feeble,
they became rarer still.

.

One day, however, in the dirty living-room of
his cottage, Le Mesurier sat and entertained an
unexpected and most unwelcome guest.

Outside the window nothing was visible but
whiteness — an opaque, luminous, sun-suffused
whiteness, which obliterated earth and sky and
sea. For Le Tas, and Saint Maclou, and the
whole Island Archipelago, were enveloped in one

of those wet and hurrying mists so common here in August. It blew from the north-east; broke against the high cliffs of Saint Maclou, as a river breaks against a boulder; overflowed the top; filled up every valley, transforming each into the semblance of a stagnant lake; and, pouring down every headland on the south and west, swept out again to sea.

The cottage on Le Tas, at all times solitary, was this afternoon completely cut off from the rest of the world.

Le Mesurier's living-room, in its dirt and its disorder, showed plainly that no woman ever came there. Unwashed cooking utensils and crockery littered up the hearth and dresser; the baize cover and cushions of the *jonquière*, often laid upon, were never shaken or cleaned; rusting guns, disordered fishing tackle, canvases, a battered oil-paint box, spoke of occupations thrown aside and tastes forgotten. On a table in the window were writing materials; a couple of dog-eared books; a tobacco-jar, a pipe, and a bottle of whisky. These last, of all the articles in the room, alone showed the lustre which comes from frequent use.

The host's appearance matched his surround-ings. He wore a dirty flannel shirt, a ragged, paint-stained coat, burst canvas shoes. His hands were unwashed, his hair and beard were un-

I

combed, and neither had been touched by scissors
for the last six months.

The guest, on the contrary, was clean, fragrant,
irreproachable at every point; in a light grey
summer suit and brown boots; with glossy linen,
and glossy, well-kept finger-nails. He had a trick
of drawing these together in an even row over
the palm of his hand, while he contemplated
them admiringly, his head a little on one side.
The dabs of light reflected from their surface
made them look like a row of polished pink shells.
Le Mesurier remembered this trick of old, and
hated Shergold for it, but not more than he hated
him for everything else.

Shergold, on his arrival, had asked for something to eat. Le Mesurier had taken bread and
cheese from the cupboard, and flinging them
down on the table before him, had filled a great
tin jug—one of the curious tin jugs never seen
elsewhere than in the Islands—with cider from
the cask in the corner.

"Yes," Shergold was saying, "we were two
hours late; and, but that old Hamon piloted us,
we might never have got here at all. I don't
believe any one but Hamon could have kept us
off the rocks to-day. I only hope we shall make
better time going back, or I shall lose the boat for
Jersey. That would mean staying in Jacques-le-
Port until Monday, and I'm anxious to get to Lily

at once.   She will be so glad to know I have seen you, to hear all about you."

Le Mesurier's dull, quiescent hate sprang suddenly into activity. He felt he could have throttled the man who sat so calmly on the other side of the table, eating, and speaking between his mouthfuls of Le Mesurier's wife. He could have throttled him for the unctuous correctness of his appearance, for his conventional, meaningless good looks, for those empty, showy eyes of his, which the fools who believed in him called "flashing" and "intellectual"; he could have throttled him for the air of self-satisfaction, of complacency, breathed by his whole person; he could have throttled him for the amiable lie he had just told of Lily's anxiety for news of himself, her husband. All Lily was anxious to hear, of course, was that Shergold had obtained Le Mesurier's consent to the business proposition over which they had been corresponding for so long, and which to-day was the occasion of Shergold's visit.

But he concealed his rage, and only showed his surprise on hearing that Lily was again in Jersey. For one of the many subjects of disagreement between her and himself, one of their many causes of quarrel, had been her persistent detestation of Jersey.

Shergold explained: "Yes. I hadn't time to mention it in my last letter; but Lily left London

on Monday, and has gone to some very nice
rooms I was able to secure for her at Beaumont.
In fact, my old rooms—you will remember them
—when I was at the College."

"She might at least have gone home," said Le
Mesurier, with bitterness, "since I'm not there to
contaminate the place. Rozaine, as she knows, is
always at her service."

"Ah, yes—of course—thank you—you are very
kind. But the air of Rozaine is hardly sufficiently
bracing. You see, it's on account of the boy.
He has been overworking at his studies, and needs
sea-bathing, tonic, ozone."

The impertinence of Shergold's thanks might
have stung Le Mesurier to an angry retort, but
that the mention of his little son, whom he had
not seen for more than a year, gave his thoughts
and feelings a different bent. He caught himself wishing he could have him out here on
Le Tas. The keen air, the free, out-of-door,
wholesome life, would soon put health into the
body, and colour into the pale little face, that
rose so vividly before the father's mind. Another
of the causes of dissension between Le Mesurier
and Lily had been the system, inspired by Shergold, which she had rigorously insisted upon
following in the training and education of the
child. Every day had its regular set programme
of lessons and of play; but the play consisted

of formal exercise—"Calisthenics," as Shergold
termed it—which at stated hours the boy was
obliged to accomplish ; so that, to his constrained
young spirit, it no doubt became as irksome as a
task. And then, Shergold, though a hearty con-
sumer of butcher's meat in practice, was, in
theory, a convinced vegetarian ; and Lily, despite
her husband's most earnest, most violent opposition, would allow little Phil no stronger nourish-
ment than such as might be contained in beans
and lentils.

Le Mesurier spoke aloud, impulsively. "Lily
might send Phil to me for a few weeks, I think.
It would do him all the good in the world. It is
much healthier here than at Beaumont."

Shergold raised his eyebrows, and took a com-
prehensive glance round the unswept, uncleaned,
undusted room.

"Oh, I'd have a woman in. I'd have all this set
right," said the father, eagerly.

"You can hardly be serious," answered Shergold. "You know Lily's views. You could
hardly expect her to let Phil stop here alone with
you."

Le Mesurier flushed angrily.

"After all, he's my own child. If I chose to
assert my rights—if I should insist on having
him——"

"Oh, your rights !" interrupted Shergold.

"Come, come. You're forgetting our agreement. The boy remains in his mother's care, and under her control, till he's one-and-twenty, and you're not to interfere."

"But it was understood that I could see him whenever I wished."

"And so you can. But you must go to see him ; Lily can't let him leave her to come to you. If you choose to exile yourself to Le Tas, and to lead this solitary, half-savage sort of life, you can't complain that you're prevented from seeing Phil. It's your own fault. You ought to be living at Rozaine."

"Tell my wife what she ought or ought not to do, since she's fool enough to listen to you," broke out Le Mesurier hotly, "and be damned to you both ! I shall do as I please. What business is it of yours where or how I live ?"

Shergold shrugged his shoulders.

"You appear to be as violent in temper, and as unrestrained in language, as ever," he said calmly. "A pretty example you'd set your son ! But we're straying from the point. Let us give our attention to the business that brought me here, and get it done with." He drew a large envelope from the inner breast-pocket of his coat.

"You may save yourself the trouble of opening that," Le Mesurier informed him. "Tell Lily to send me the boy for a month, and I'll consider the matter. Under present conditions, I refuse even to discuss it with you."

Shergold sat and surveyed his host with an exasperating mixture of curiosity, contempt, and reprobation. "You are talking nonsense," he said presently. "You know she won't send you the boy. The notion is preposterous. Now, as for these papers——"

"I refuse to discuss the matter," Le Mesurier repeated. "Send me Phil, and we'll see. But, until then, I refuse to discuss it. If Lily hesitates, use your influence with her," he added sardonically. "The notion's preposterous, if you like, but you've persuaded her to more preposterous courses still, before now. You've persuaded her to leave her husband, to give up her position, her duties; you've persuaded her to go and live in London, to be near you, to complete her education, to develop her individuality, and a lot of damned rot of that sort. Well, now, persuade her to this. Persuade her to let me have the boy for a time. Persuade her that it's for Phil's own good. And tell her roundly that I refuse absolutely to hold any kind of business discussions with either her or her agent, until she agrees."

Shergold's voice acquired a touch of acerbity. "You're mad, Le Mesurier," he said. "It is I, as you know, who have always consistently advised

Lily to remove the boy as far as possible from
your influence. If you are serious in asking me
now to urge her to let him come here, and live
alone with you, day in and day out, for a month—
upon my soul, you must be mad."

"Very good. Mad or not, you have heard my
last word. And if you cannot see your way to
meeting my wishes in the matter, I don't know
that there's anything that need detain you here
longer."

He looked significantly from Shergold to the
door. The mist was lifting a little. The sun was
just visible behind it, a patin of pale gold shining
through the filmy veil of the sanctuary ; here and
there, at a distance from the sun, long rifts were
torn in the veil, disclosing a background of faint
blue sky.

Shergold, vexed, hesitant, looked at his watch.

"You're wasting precious time," he said impatiently. "What's the use of opening old sores ?
You know our decision about the child is irrevo-
cably fixed. You yourself assented to it long ago.
What's the sense of letting this new idea of yours
—this freak—this whim, to have him here—interfere with business of importance—business about
which I've taken the trouble to pay you this altogether distasteful visit ? "

But Le Mesurier merely opened the door, and
with a gesture invited Shergold to pass out. His

expression was so menacing, his gesture might so
easily have transformed itself into the preparation
for a blow, that Shergold instinctively moved towards the threshold.

" You refuse to consider the matter ? " he asked.

" Let Lily send the boy, and I'll consider it."

" That's your last word ? "

" No ! " shouted Le Mesurier, suddenly losing
all control of himself. "Go to Hell, you sneaking
Jesuit ! That's my last word." Then, finding a
certain childish joy in the mere calling of names
—the mere utterance of his hate, his fury : " You
empty wind-bag ! You low-bred pedant ! You
bloated mass of self-conceit ! Go to Hell ! "

And he flung the door to, in Shergold's astonished face.

* * *

Le Mesurier stood alone in the cottage, shaken
by impotent rage. His thoughts followed Shergold
going away ; unsuccessful, indeed, but superior,
calm, self-satisfied ; full of a lofty contempt, a
Pharisaic pity, for Le Mesurier's violence, for his
childishness, his ineffectual profanity, his miserable
mode of life. Le Mesurier could imagine Shergold
telling Lily of her husband's churlish refusal to
discuss the business that had taken him to Saint
Maclou ; of the impossible condition he had
imposed ; of his dirty surroundings, his neglected

appearance, his brutal language, his ungovernable temper.   Le Mesurier saw the disgust such a narration would inspire in his wife, the fresh justification she would find in it for all her past conduct. And he imagined how, while Shergold and Lily talked him over, Phil, the child, his son, would catch a word here and there, as children do, and would unconsciously conceive a prejudice against his father, which would influence him through life. . . . God ! it was unendurable. Was there no way ? . . . .

Then, all at once, he laughed. An idea had begun to push its head insidiously up from among the confusion of his thoughts. This idea surprised him, pleased him, tempted him ; and, as he contemplated it, he laughed. . . .

In a moment he opened the door and hurried out, after Shergold.

The sun was again hidden, the blue rifts had closed, the mist was thicker than before. But, a little distance ahead, a dark form was silhouetted on the whiteness ; and, thrilling with excitement, in a glow of irresponsible gaiety, Le Mesurier, following noiselessly over the grass, kept this form in view.

Along the meandering foot-worn track, which leads from the Barracks back over Le Tas ; down through the gorse and bracken ; on through the lane that skirts the tree-sheltered cottages ; and so to the beginning of the Coupée, where the land falls away, and nothing is left but the narrow road that creeps tremulously over the top of the rock wall, three hundred feet high, with a precipice on either side, and the sea at the bottom : Le Mesurier stealthily followed Shergold.

And when the middle of the Coupée was reached, Le Mesurier knew that the moment had come. He acted promptly. Before there was time for speech between the men, the thing was done, and he stood there on the road alone — a startled broken cry still ringing in his ears ; then, after what seemed a long interval of silence, a splash, a far-away muffled splash, from deep below, as if he had dropped a stone, wrapped in a blanket, into the water.

Le Mesurier waited till the silence grew round and complete again. Then he turned away light-heartedly, and walked back to Le Tas.

II

HE was glad that his enemy was dead.

This was the thought, this the feeling—a feeling of gladness, a thought, "But I am glad, glad, glad!"—which kept him company all the succeeding days.

The knowledge that he would never have to see him again—never again look upon his fatuous, handsome face—never again listen to his voice, his smooth, equable, complacent voice — this knowledge poured through him with warm comfort.

He would lie out on the grass, in the sun, revelling in a sensation of well-being that was almost physical, and rehearsing in memory the events as they had happened : Shergold's arrival, their conversation, Shergold's departure ; the great, good, satisfying outburst of vituperation with which Le Mesurier had pursued him from his threshold ; and then that brief moment of soul-filling consummation, of tangible, ponderable joy, on the Coupée.

Remorse ?   No, he did not feel the slightest remorse.   "Remorse ?—I thought a man who had killed another always felt remorse," he said to himself, with a vague sort of surprise, but with very certain exultation.   Hitherto, he had accepted tacitly the conventional teachings on the subject.   Bloodguiltiness must be followed by remorse, as certainly as night by morning. The slayer destroyed, along with his victim, his own peace for ever.   He could no more enjoy food, rest, or pleasant indolence.   And sleep— "Macbeth has murdered sleep !"   He must always be haunted by the reproachful phantom of the dead, shaken by continual ague-fits of terror, gnawed by perpetual dread, lest his crime should be discovered and brought home to him. These were the ready-made notions the truth of which Le Mesurier had taken for granted : but now he had tested them; he had tested them, and behold, they were false.   After all, he told him-self, every man's experience is individual ; you can learn nothing from books, nothing from the experience of others.   Hearsay evidence is worth-less.   "I am a murderer, as it is called.   I should inevitably be hanged if they could prove the thing against me.   And yet—remorse ?"   No ; he felt himself to be a thousand times happier, a thousand times easier in his mind, a thousand times more contented, more at peace, than he had

ever been in the days of his innocence. In killing
Shergold, he had simply removed an intolerable
burden from his spirit.

He found himself singing, whistling, scraps of
opera, snatches of old ballads, as he went about
the daily routine of preparing his food, or as he
wandered hither and thither over the scant sun-
burned grass of the islet. After all, Shergold had
well deserved his fate. It was owing to him that
Le Mesurier's life was ruined, his home broken
up, his boy separated from him, his wife's affections alienated. It was thanks to Shergold that
he had come here, more than a year ago, to lead
the life of a misanthrope, alone in this melancholy
cottage on Le Tas.

And yet, Shergold was not his wife's lover ;
had never been her lover ; never, Le Mesurier
knew, had desired to be her lover. He thought
he could almost have forgiven Shergold more
easily if he *had* been her lover ; the situation
would have seemed, somehow, less abnormal
than the actual one. But Shergold had got at her
intellectually, had seduced her mind, had subjugated her spiritually. He had known her before
her marriage, ever since she was a girl of sixteen.
He had given her lessons in Greek, in mathe-
matics. Possibly, had he not been a married
man himself at the time, he might have thought
of marrying her. But it was after her marriage

to Le Mesurier, after Shergold's own wife's death, about a year afterwards, that his ascendancy over her became marked, that his constant presence at Rozaine began vaguely to irritate the husband.

He was such a cold, self-righteous, solemn, pompous pedant, and withal such an ass, so shallow, so empty, so *null*. His pose of mental superiority was so unwarranted, so odious. Yet he betrayed in a hundred inflections of his voice, in perpetual supercilious upliftings of his eyebrows, the contempt he entertained for Le Mesurier, as for a mere eating, drinking, sport-loving animal, without culture, without fineness, without acquirements, but unfairly endowed by Fortune with large estates and a charming wife; a wife who, in other hands, with a wise and discerning helpmeet, might (to use one of Shergold's own irritating catch-words) "have raised the pyramid of self-culture to the highest point." Shergold imagined himself to be like Goethe, to resemble him physically, as well as temperamentally, and in the character of his mind; and he was constantly adopting, and adapting to the exigencies of the moment, tag-ends of the poet's phrases. He had a deep-seated, intimate conviction—a conviction based not on evidence, not on experience, not on work accomplished, but born, full-fledged, of his own instinctive egotism—that he was, not merely a clever man, not merely a man of uncommon parts, but a Great Man, a Man of transcendent Genius. It was as a Man of Genius that Lily Le Mesurier looked up to him ; it was as a Man of Genius that he looked down upon Lily Le Mesurier's husband. And yet Philip, modest enough, and unpretentious, could not help realising in his heart, that, of the two, he himself was, in point of real native intelligence, the better man.

Shergold displayed a silent commiseration for Lily which infuriated Le Mesurier. He taught her to commiserate herself. She turned to him for sympathy in all her imagined troubles ; she sought his advice on every point. She put the management of the child virtually into his hands. He was always at Rozaine. He came up there every day, directly his duties at the College left him free. Lily kept him to dinner three or four times a week. If Le Mesurier grumbled, she complained that he grudged her her only amusement—good conversation ; that, save Professor Shergold, she never met any one worth listening to, worth talking to. He was the only man who understood her. Life was dull enough, Heaven knew, at Rozaine ; and, if Philip was going to object to the Professor's visits, she would not be able to live there at all. It was an effective threat, the value of which Lily thoroughly appreciated, a threat she did not scruple to employ as often as occasion demanded, that she would "not be able to go on living at Rozaine;" for Le Mesurier had a dumb passion for the place, and an immense pride in it: it was his home, his birthplace, it had been in his family for generations. His love for Lily was a passion too. To live at Rozaine with her—with children possibly—he had pictured to himself as the ideal of absolute happiness. He could as little imagine himself living anywhere else, as he could imagine himself living without Lily. So what could he do but submit, and confirm Lily's constant invitations to Shergold, with such cordiality as he could feign, and sit silent at the head of his table, while these two talked radicalism, agnosticism, blatant futilities, cheap enthusiasms of all sorts ? The Emancipation of Woman, the Abolition of Monarchy, State Socialism, Disestablishment. . . . And Le Mesurier was conservative, as all the Islanders are, and religious as men go. That is to say, he honoured the Church in which he had been brought up, and in which all those whom he had cared for had lived and died.

It troubled him, therefore, that, when little Phil began to talk, Lily protested against the child's being taught any prayers. The Professor, she said, held it criminal to fill a child's mind with discredited theologies. No mention of the Christian Myth should be permitted in his presence till

K

he was old enough to judge, to discriminate for himself. " It was just as criminal as it would be to offer him innutritious or deleterious food for his physical sustenance," Shergold explained. When Phil was three years old, Le Mesurier put his foot down, and declared that the child must be brought up a Christian. There was a great scene, at the end of which Le Mesurier's anger exploded in curses ; and Lily seized the opportunity for the appropriate sneer that " if that sort of language was Christian, she preferred the language of Atheists." Shergold urged, " But my dear fellow ! Be reasonable. You don't want to teach your son demoralising superstitions. The existence of a God, the divinity of Jesus of Nazareth—I can prove to you the absurdity of both in five minutes, if you will listen. It's monstrous to instil such unscientific and pernicious dogmas into the brain of a three-year-old infant." Le Mesurier took Phil on his knee, alone in the nursery, and taught him the simple prayer he himself had used as a child.

After their discussion, and Le Mesurier's burst of profanity, Shergold had left the house in injured dignity ; and Lily had retired to her room, and remained there for forty-eight hours. At the end of that time Le Mesurier was reduced to submission. Lily insisted on his going down to the College, and bringing the Professor back to dinner. The old footing was resumed, and things went from bad to infinitely worse. Every periodic outbreak on Le Mesurier's part was more violent than the last, and every reparation exacted from him was more galling. The legend of his violence, of his ill-conduct, began to spread about the Island, and to form one of the chosen themes of gossip at the club, and at St. Hélier's tea-parties. The absolutely platonic nature of the Professor's relations with Lily seemed to be understood, for in a place where scandal is peculiarly rife, their friendship never excited any.

In the course of six years Le Mesurier had become a cypher in his own house, and Shergold ruled by suggestion in small things as well as in great. Le Mesurier covered an intolerable hatred with a sullen and morose manner, and had endured with apparent insensibility many keener mortifications than the one which finally brought matters to a crisis.

He had come home tired one day from the golf links, and found Shergold, as usual, discoursing to Lily in the drawing-room. Le Mesurier threw himself into an easy chair, conscious of no more than his habitual annoyance. The drawing-room tea had been taken away, and it wanted about half-an-hour to dinner. Shergold commented on his fagged appearance, and offered him refreshment.

"Come now, do take a glass of wine," he said, "or some brandy and soda ;" with all the cordial civility of a man dispensing hospitality from his own hearth-rug. "Let me ring for it."

But before he could touch the bell, Le Mesurier was on his feet, his temper boiling over, his mouth spluttering forth indignant protestations. The infernal insolence of the man, to play the host to him in his own house ! " By God," he cried, " I think this really is the limit ! "

The Professor, always coldly superior, and deaf to Lily's entreaties where his own dignity was at stake, took up his hat, and left the room. A moment later he was passing before the windows on his way to the lodge-gates.

Then came a scene with Lily, more shattering than anything Le Mesurier could have imagined. In her cool little voice, she said the cruellest things. Her tongue cut like the lash of a cunningly contrived whip, and she brought it down again and again on the most sensitive places of his soul ; those secret places which no mere enemy could have discovered, but which, because of his love for her, he had exposed fearlessly to her mercy. His pain turned to anger : his anger became really a brief madness. He had suddenly found himself standing over her, holding her by the shoulder, shaking her violently. " Damn you,

you little devil !" he had shouted, and his fingers
had thrilled to strike her on her pale provocative
face ; but instinct, rather than deliberate forbear-
ance, had saved him from this, and he had gripped
her shoulder instead.   Then at that very moment
the door had opened, and Wilkins had entered to
announce dinner.   She had stood and looked at
him with narrowing, malignant eyes—God, those
eyes he had so worshipped !—"You need not
strike me before the servants," she had said, just
as though he had been in the habit of striking her,
and she had raised her clear voice a little, obviously
that the man might hear.   Le Mesurier had hastily
moved back a step, but his cuff-link had caught in
the gauzy stuff that filled in the neck of her dress,
and a portion of it had torn away, and hung in a
long fluttering strip from his sleeve.   She had
made no movement to cover her bare neck ; on
the contrary, she pushed up her shoulder through
the gap, and turned her eyes, now tender, grieving
eyes, to look at the five angry crimson marks
rising up on the white skin.   Wilkins, of course,
had seen them plainly too.   She had refused to go
in to dinner, she had gone to her room ; when,
later, Le Mesurier went there to ask forgive-
ness, he could not find her.   The boy's crib in
the next room was empty.   His wife had left
Rozaine, and taken the child with her.   She had
gone to an hotel in St. Hélier's for the night, and

left for her father's house in England the next
morning.

She had steadfastly refused to return, and
Shergold had supported her in her refusal. He
had shortly after this given up his appointment
at St. Hélier's for a better one in London, where
he had lived near Lily, influencing her as much
as ever, seeing her, doubtless, every day. In the
few letters which Lily had written her husband
since the separation—letters dealing always with
points of business, with money arrangements,
rendered necessary by their altered relations—
Le Mesurier recognised, in the cold, judicial tone,
the well-arranged phrases, Shergold's guiding
hand. He at first had answered them briefly,
latterly not at all, and it was his final persistent
silence which had brought his enemy in person
to Le Tas, and delivered him into his hands.—
Oh, he was glad he had killed him! Shergold
had ruined his life, and he had taken Shergold's.
They were quits at last. No, he felt no remorse.

* *
*

But neither did he feel any fear; and this surprised him, for that the transgressor should fear
discovery and retribution was within every man's
experience. He began to ask himself how this
was, and he came to believe that it arose from the
fact that he had in reality no cause for fear.

Discovery was practically an impossibility. In the first place, no one knew that Shergold had come to Saint Maclou at all. He had told Le Mesurier it was a sudden idea which had occurred to him during dinner, on which he had acted the same night. Then the boat had been so late, that, to save time, he had not gone into the hotel, where he might have been remembered, but had come up to Le Tas over the cliffs, without notice or recognition from anybody. That he should have been seen between leaving the cottage and reaching the Coupée was impossible. Le Mesurier had followed him closely enough all the way to know that no one else had been at any time in sight. And so thick was the mist, that a third person, to have seen him at all, must have passed within arm's length. From all danger of an eyewitness to his being in Shergold's company, or to the supreme moment on the Coupée, Le Mesurier felt secure.

But there was the chance that the body might be recovered. It might be washed up on the Island or elsewhere. The body of young Hamon, who had fallen from the cliffs the previous summer, while searching for gulls' eggs, had been found three weeks later, so far away as the Isle of Wight. It had been unrecognisable, for the face was completely destroyed, but it had been identified by a pocket-knife with the lad's name

engraved upon the haft. Le Mesurier wondered
whether there was anything on Shergold's person
to identify him. Letters ? The water would have
reduced these to pulp. A ring ? The hands and
fingers were always the parts first attacked by the
fish.

He recalled the gruesome stories told by the
boatmen as they row you from point to point, or
which the women repeat to each other during the
long winter evenings as they sit over the peat
fires : stories fo the cave-crabs, of the voracious
fish which swarm round these coasts ; of the
mackerel which come in shoals, hundreds of
thousands strong, roughening the calm sea like a
wind, making a noise like thunder or the engines
of some great steamer, as they cut through the
surface of the water in pursuit of the little fish
that fly before them. One story goes that a man
swimming out from Grève de la Mauve un-
wittingly struck into such a shoal, and in an
instant was pulled down by a million tenacious
mouths and never seen again. . . . No, there was
not much fear that Shergold's body would be
found.

But even supposing the body were found and
were recognised ; even supposing Shergold's
movements could be traced to Saint Maclou, that
his visit to Le Mesurier could be proved ; there
was no iota of evidence to connect Le Mesurier

with his death. Le Mesurier's policy would be
frankly to acknowledge the visit, to describe how
Shergold had left him, and to call to remembrance the mist which had prevailed on that day.
What more natural than that Shergold should
have met with a misadventure on the way back,
have walked over the cliff's edge instead of keeping to the path, have missed his footing and fallen
from the Coupée? Such misadventures were
constantly happening, even among the fishermen.
There was not a point on the Island which was
not already the scene of some such tragedy. Le
Mesurier assured himself he had no cause for
fear.

* * *

But as the days and weeks went by, what did
surprise him exceedingly was that he received no
communication from Lily to acquaint him with
the Professor's disappearance. It had seemed
certain that she would write. For long ago
Shergold must have been missed; first by his
landlady, then by his friends. There would have
been much speculation, anxious inquiries, newspaper paragraphs, in which his person would be
described, a reward offered. Then, as time went
on, and nothing was heard of him, the anxiety
must have grown. There must have been an
immense noise, a tremendous amount of talk.

For he was, in his way, a well-known man, a person of consideration ; he held a responsible post. Le Mesurier never saw a newspaper ; not more than a dozen, perhaps, were read in the whole of Saint Maclou, and these were chiefly local papers from Jacques-le-Port ; but he could imagine the excitement of the London press, the articles which were being written on the subject, the letters, the suggestions, which every day must be bringing forth.

And nevertheless, Le Mesurier received no notification from Lily ; no news of any sort, no rumour touching Shergold's fate was ever carried to Le Tas. The strangeness of such a silence could only confirm him in the belief that Shergold had spoken to no one of his intended journey to Saint Maclou, and he again told himself he was absolutely safe. He set himself to dismiss the subject from his mind.

But he found to his astonishment that he could not dismiss it, that it had become a fixed idea, an obsession, which overpowered his will. He was as impotent to chase Shergold from his waking thoughts as from his troubled nightly dreams. If he looked up suddenly to the window, it was because he fancied he had seen Shergold's head passing rapidly by; if he caught himself listening intently in the stillness, he knew a moment later that it was because he fancied Shergold had spoken, and that the vibrations of his voice still shook the air. It was a horrible disappointment to discover that instead of ridding himself of Shergold, as he had hoped, he seemed to have bound himself up with him inseparably for ever. While he had been alive, Le Mesurier, once out of his presence, had often forgotten him for days at a time; now that he was dead, Le Mesurier could think of nothing else.

* * *

But a more curious development was, that as time went by, he noticed that his old, hearty, satisfying hatred for the man was fading away. Does not absence invariably weaken hatred? And when you realise that absence to be the eternal, to be the immutable absence of death, is not hatred thereby extinguished? Love is stronger than death, for love is positive, affirmative. But hatred? Hatred is negative; hatred is a manifestation of the transitory Nay, not of the everlasting Yea. Is it possible to hate the dead?

Le Mesurier no longer hated the man he had killed. A faint, hesitant sort of consideration, even of fellow-feeling for him, began gradually to edge its way in among his thoughts. He would actually sometimes try to put himself in Shergold's place; he would try to reconstruct the past from Shergold's point of view.

He found he could no longer persuade himself
that Shergold had been conscious of the evil he
had wrought. On the contrary, he recognised
that the man had been honest according to his
lights; that he had committed no crime against
the accepted code. He might have acquired his
influence over Lily, through no wish, no effort
of his own. He had been one of those showy
characters whom women always worship; he had
possessed that superficial glittering cleverness that
always catches a woman's fancy; he had talked
with the fluent self-assurance which always wins
a woman's approval. Probably he had never
realised how obnoxious his presence at Rozaine
was to Le Mesurier. He was sufficiently proud
to have withdrawn from a society where he was
not wanted, but his self-conceit was too magnificent for him ever to imagine such a contingency
possible. And then, no doubt, his sense of conscious rectitude had rendered him particularly
obtuse. Had he been playing the rôle of lover, a
guilty conscience would have made him more
sensitive to Le Mesurier's uncordial attitude.
Looking back upon it all now, Le Mesurier could
almost pity him for such blindness.

* * *

One day, lying in a hollow of the cliff, hidden
from every eye but that of cormorant or sea-gull,

playing abstractedly with a pebble which found
itself under his fingers, he saw a yard away from
him a sharp-nosed, grey-coated mole running
from one point to another across the grass. He
shot the pebble from his hand, and the little beast
rolled over dead. He took it up, and looked at it
curiously. He smoothed with his fingers its warm,
velvety coat. He was sorry he had killed it. A
second ago it had been enjoying the sunshine, the
warm air, its own sense of well-being. And now
it was utterly destroyed, utterly annihilated, and
no one could restore to it the life which he had
wantonly taken.

The thought of Shergold at once pressed
forward imperatively. Shergold had not believed
in soul or immortality. He had believed that
with death the life of a man comes to an end,
just as does the life of a mouse. Le Mesurier
had often listened, perforce, to his dogmatising
on such views to Lily ; to his proclaiming
that each individual life is but a flash of light
between two eternities of darkness ; that just as
the body returns to the elements from which it
came, so the spirit is reabsorbed into the forces
and energies which move the world. And because
Shergold had no belief in another life, he had
set an immense value upon this one. In his
self-engrossed, pedantic way, he had thoroughly
enjoyed every hour, every moment of it. Sup-

posing his views were true, then the greatest injury one could inflict on such a man would be to deprive him of this life which he prized, suddenly to extinguish him like a candle, to annihilate him like this poor little mole.

Le Mesurier laid the body of the mole down upon the turf, and walked away. He no longer sang or whistled to himself. The monotonous days seemed intolerably long.

III

THREE months had gone by. Le Mesurier, in the solitude of Le Tas, had suffered every pang a guilty conscience can inflict, had lived through every phase of remorse and of despair.

The burden on his mind was growing intolerably heavy. Every moment it cried out to him that he must share it with another, or be crushed beneath its weight. He would have gone down to see the Pastor, but that to do so he must cross the Coupée. He had not the physical courage to pass the spot from which his thoughts were never long absent. And while his mind tossed distressfully this way and that, Monsieur Chauchat chanced to come up to see him.

The sight of a real human face, the sound of a real human voice, unlocked his heart, set his tongue going. In spite of the old man's many attempted interruptions, he poured out the whole story; all the injuries, real or fancied, he had received at Shergold's hands, his own hatred for him, the man's fate, his own impotent repentance.

"And now," he said, simply, when he had concluded, " I wish to give myself up. Tell me what
I am to do."

Chauchat looked at him with infinite pity, and
showed neither horror nor surprise. Le Mesurier
was even conscious of a certain movement of
indignation within his own bosom, that any one
should hear of the murder of a fellow-creature
so composedly.

" You must give up this kind of life," said the
pastor gently. " It is terribly bad for you. You
must have society, you must travel."

Le Mesurier was amazed at such irrelevance.
He looked at Chauchat curiously. He thought
him aged, whiter, feebler than ever before. He
wondered whether he still had all his faculties.
And he answered impatiently, " But what has that
to do with what I have been telling you ?"

"You must take care," said the old man ;
"solitude brings delusions, hallucinations; to indulge in them is to shake the mind's stability.
You must come back into the world. You must
mix with other men."

He divined that Chauchat believed him to be
dreaming. This was natural perhaps ; how could
the good, simple-minded old clergyman believe in
the reality of such a crime ? But he must convince him of the miserable truth. He must begin
again and describe it all more circumstantially.

He must go on until he saw conviction dawn
in the eyes that now looked at him with such
friendly pity, until he saw that pity change to
aversion and fear.   He began over again.

But Chauchat laid a hand upon his arm.

" One moment ! You say you killed this man ? "

" Yes, I killed him."

" You threw him over the Coupée ? "

" I followed him from the house, and threw
him over the Coupée."

" No, my poor boy ; no, no, no !   Thank God,
you did not.   Thank God, you are dreaming.
You have had some strange, some horrible
delusion.   For Shergold is alive, is well, I have
but just now come from him.   He, indeed, is
the reason of my visit.   I come as a messenger
from him, a mediator between him and you."

Le Mesurier sat there stunned, dazed, vacant.
Was Chauchat mad ?   The old man's voice buzzed
in his ears ; he was still talking, explaining how
Shergold had come over by the morning's boat ;
how he had called at the parsonage, and told the
story of his last visit to Le Mesurier, of the deed
of assignment, and of Le Mesurier's refusal to sign
it ; of the pressing need there was that it should be
signed ; how he had begged Chauchat to use his
influence with Le Mesurier, and so Chauchat was
here, while Shergold was staying till to-morrow at
the Belle Vue Hotel, and was quite prepared to

L

meet Le Mesurier on amicable terms, if he would go down there and see him.

Was Chauchat mad ? Yes, clearly. How otherwise could he imagine that he had come from Shergold, that he had spoken with a dead man ? Shergold's death—that was the one certain fact in all this bewildering world. He had sat there, at the table, just where Chauchat was seated now. They had quarrelled. Le Mesurier had followed him from that very door, out into the mist . . .

But all at once a point of doubt pierced his soul. *Had* he followed Shergold ? Had he in truth followed Shergold out into the mist ?

Was Chauchat mad . . . or . . . or was he mad himself ? Something inside his head throbbed so violently, he could not even think. He sat stunned and dazed by the table holding his head in his hands, while the old man talked on. But while he sat there in dumb, inert confusion, his subconscious brain was at work, rearranging the past, disentangling the threads of illusion from those of reality, arranging these on this side, those on that, clearly, unmistakably. And when all was ready, suddenly the web of deception fell from before his eyes, and he saw clearly. Up to the moment of Shergold's leaving the cottage all had passed as he remembered it : the rest had been a mere phantasmal creation of his own brain.

His hands were clean of blood, he had committed no crime, he might go where he chose, he was guiltless, he was free . . . And during all the past months, when he had been tortured with self-condemnations, Shergold had been living his usual happy, respectable and respected life, seeing Lily every day, seeing the child . . . God ! God ! . . . Le Mesurier's feelings underwent a complete revulsion ; his remorse shrivelled up, his pity vanished, his old hatred returned reinforced a thousandfold—and he was filled with regret, with a poignant, an intolerable regret, that his hand had failed to accomplish the sin which his heart had desired.

THE DEATH MASK

THE DEATH MASK

THE Master was dead; and Peschi, who had come round to the studio to see about some repairs—part of the ceiling had fallen owing to the too lively proceedings of Dubourg and his eternal visitors overhead — Peschi displayed a natural pride that it was he who had been selected from among the many *mouleurs* of the Quarter, to take a mask of the dead man.

All Paris was talking of the Master, although not, assuredly, under that title. All Paris was talking of his life, of his genius, of his misery, and of his death. Peschi, for the moment, was sole possessor of valuable unedited details, to the narration of which Hiram P. Corner, who had dropped in to pass the evening with me, listened with keenly attentive ears.

Corner was a recent addition to the American Art Colony; ingenuous as befitted his eighteen years, and of a more than improbable innocence. Paris, to him, represented the Holiest of Holies;

the dead Master, by the adorable impeccability of his writings, figuring therein as one of the High Priests. Needless to say, he had never come in contact with that High Priest, had never even seen him ; while the Simian caricatures which so frequently embellished the newspapers, made as little impression on the lad's mind, as did the equivocal allusions, jests, and epigrams, for ever flung up like sea-spray against the rock of his unrevered name.

The absorbing interest Corner felt glowed visibly on his fresh young western face, and it was this, I imagine, which led Peschi to propose that we should go back with him to his *atelier* and see the mask for ourselves.

Peschi is a Genoese ; small, lithe, very handsome ; a skilled workman, a little demon of industry ; full of enthusiasms, with the real artist-soul. He works for Felon the sculptor, and it was Felon who had been commissioned to do the bust for which the death mask would serve as model.

It is always pleasant to hear Peschi talk ; and to-night, as we walked from the Rue Fleurus to the Rue Notre-Dame-des-Champs, he told us something of mask-taking in general, with illustrations from this particular case.

On the preceding day, barely two hours after death had taken place, Rivereau, one of the dead

man's intimates, had rushed into Peschi's work-
room, and carried him off, with the necessary
materials, to the Rue Monsieur, in a cab. Rivereau,
though barely twenty, is perhaps the most notorious
of the *bande*. Peschi described him to Corner
as having dark, evil, narrow eyes set too close
together in a perfectly white face, framed by falling, lustreless black hair ; and with the stooping
shoulders, the troubled walk, the attenuated hands
common to his class.

Arrived at the house, Rivereau led the way up
the dark and dirty staircase to the topmost land-
ing, and as they paused there an instant, Peschi
could hear the long-drawn, hopeless sob of a
woman within the door.

On being admitted he found himself in an
apartment consisting of two small, inconceivably
squalid rooms, opening one from the other.

In the outer room, five or six figures, the
disciples, friends, and lovers of the dead poet,
conversed together ; a curious group in a medley
of costumes. One in an opera-hat, shirt-sleeves,
and soiled grey trousers tied up with a bit of stout
string ; another in a black coat buttoned high to
conceal the fact that he wore no shirt at all; a
third in clothes crisp from the tailor, with an
immense bunch of Parma violets in his button-
hole. But all were alike in the strangeness of
their eyes, their voices, their gestures.

Seen through the open door of the further room, lay the corpse under a sheet, and by the bedside knelt the stout, middle-aged mistress, whose sobs had reached the stairs.

Madame Germaine, as she was called in the Quarter, had loved the Master with that complete, self-abnegating, sublime love of which certain women are capable—a love uniting that of the mother, the wife, and the nurse all in one. For years she had cooked for him, washed for him, mended for him; had watched through whole nights by his bedside when he was ill; had suffered passively his blows, his reproaches, and his neglect, when, thanks to her care, he was well again. She adored him dumbly, closed her eyes to his vices, and magnified his gifts, without in the least comprehending them. She belonged to the *ouvrière* class, could not read, could not write her own name; but with a characteristic which is as French as it is un-British, she paid her homage to intellect, where an Englishwoman only gives hers to inches and muscle. Madame Germaine was prouder perhaps of the Master's greatness, worshipped him more devoutly, than any one of the super-cultivated, ultra-corrupt group, who by their flatteries and complaisances had assisted him to his ruin.

It was with the utmost difficulty, Peschi said, that Rivereau and the rest had succeeded in persuading the poor creature to leave the bedside and go into the other room while the mask was being taken.

The operation, it seems, is a sufficiently horrible one, and no relative is permitted to be present. As you cover the dead face over with the plaster, a little air is necessarily forced back again into the lungs, and this air passing along the windpipe causes strange rattlings, sinister noises, so that you might swear that the corpse was returned to life. Then, as the mould is removed, the muscles of the face drag and twitch, the mouth opens, the tongue lolls out ; and Peschi declared that this moment always remains for him a gruesome moment. He has never accustomed himself to it ; on every recurring occasion it fills him with the same repugnance, although he has taken so many masks, is so deservedly celebrated for them, that *la bande* had instantly selected him to perpetuate the Master's lineaments.

" But it's an excellent likeness," said Peschi ; "they sent for me so promptly that he had not changed at all. He does not look as though he were dead, but just asleep."

Meantime we had reached the unshuttered shop-front, where Peschi displays, on Sundays and week-days alike, his finished works of plastic art to the *gamins* and *filles* of the Quarter.

Looking past the statuary, we could see into

the living-room beyond, this being separated from the shop only by a glass partition.   The room was lighted by a lamp set in the centre of the table, and in the circle of light thrown from beneath the green lamp-shade, was enclosed a charming picture : the young head of Madame Peschi bent over her baby, whom she was feeding at the breast. She is eighteen, pretty as a rose, and her story and Peschi's is an idyllic one ; to be told, perhaps, another time.   She greeted us with the smiling, cordial, unaffected kindliness which in France warms your blood with the constant sense of brotherhood ; and, giving the boy to his father— a delicious opalescent trace of milk hanging about the little mouth—she got up to see about another lamp which Peschi had asked for.

Holding it now to guide our steps, he preceded us across a dark yard to his workshop at the further end, and while we followed him we heard the young mother's exquisite nonsense-talk addressed to the child, as she settled back in her place again to her nursing.

Peschi, unlocking a door, flashed the light down a long room, the walls of which, the trestle-tables, the very floor, were hung, laden, and encumbered with a thousand heterogeneous objects.   Casts of every description and all dimensions, finished, unfinished, broken ; scrolls for ceilings ; caryatides for chimney-pieces ; cornucopias for the entab-

latures of buildings; chubby Cupids jostling
emaciated Christs; broken columns for Père
Lachaise, or consolatory upward-pointing angels;
hands, feet, and noses for the Schools of Art; a
pensively posed *échorché* contemplating a Venus
of Milo fallen upon her back; these, and a crowd
of nameless, formless things, seemed to spring at
our eyes, as Peschi raised or lowered the lamp,
moved it this way or the other.

"There it is," said he, pointing forwards, and
I saw lying flat upon a modelling-board, with
upturned features, a grey, immobile simulacrum
of the curiously mobile face I remembered so
well.

"Of course you must understand," said Peschi,
"it's only in the rough, just exactly as it came
from the *creux*. Fifty copies are to be cast altogether, and this is the first one. But I must prop
it up for you. You can't judge of it as it is."

He looked about him for a free place on which
to set the lamp. Not finding any, he put it down
on the floor. For a few moments he stood busied
over the mask with his back to us.

"Now you can see it properly," said he, and
stepped aside.

The lamp threw its rays upwards, illuminating
strongly the lower portion of the cast, throwing the
upper portion into deepest shadow; and the effect
was that the inanimate mask became suddenly

a living face ; but a face so unutterably repulsive, so hideously bestial, that I grew cold to the roots of my hair. . . . A fat, loose throat, a retreating chinless chin, smeared and bleared with the impressions of the meagre beard ; a vile mouth, lustful, flaccid, the lower lip disproportionately great ; ignoble lines ; hateful puffinesses ; something inhuman and yet worse than inhuman in its travesty of humanity ; something that made you hate the world and your fellows, that made you hate yourself for being ever so little in *this* image. A more abhorrent spectacle I have never seen. . . .

So soon as I could turn my eyes from the ghastly thing, I looked at Corner. He was white as the plaster faces about him. His immensely opened eyes showed his astonishment and his terror. For what I experienced was intensified in his case by the unexpected and complete disillusionment. He had opened the door of the tabernacle, and out had crawled a noisome spider; he had lifted to his lips the communion cup, and therein squatted a toad. A sort of murmur of frantic protestation began to rise in his throat ; but Peschi, unconscious of our agitation, now lifted the lamp, passed round with it behind the mask, held it high, and let the rays stream downwards from above.

The astounding way the face changed must have been seen to be believed in. It was exactly

as though, by some cunning sleight of hand, the
mask of a god had been substituted for that of a
satyr. . . . You saw a splendid dome-like head,
of Socratian contour ; a broad, smooth, finely
modelled brow ; thick, regular, horizontal eyebrows, casting a shadow which diminished the
too great distance separating them from the
eyes ; while the deeper shadow thrown below the
nose altered its character entirely.   Its snout-like
appearance was gone, its deep, wide-open, upturned
nostrils were hidden ; you noticed instead the well-
marked transition from forehead to nose-base, the
broad bridge of the nose denoting extraordinary
mental power. Over the eyeballs the lids had slidden
down, smooth and creaseless ; the little tell-tale
palpebral wrinkles which had given such libidinous
lassitude to the eye had vanished away.   The lips
were no longer gross, but met each other in a
beautiful, sinuous line, now first revealed by the
shadow on the upper one.   The prominence of the
jaws, the muscularity of the lower part of the face,
which had given it so painfully microcephalous
an appearance, were now unnoticeable ; on the
contrary, the whole face looked small beneath the
noble head and brow. You remarked the medium-
sized and well-formed ears, with the " swan " dis-
tinct in each, the gently-swelling breadth of head
above them, the full development of the forehead
over the orbits of the eyes.   You discerned the

presence of those higher qualities which might
have rendered the man an ascetic or a saint ;
which led him to understand the beauty of self-
denial, to appreciate the wisdom of self-restraint :
and you did not see how these qualities remained
inoperative in him, being completely overbalanced
by the size of the lower brain, by the thick, bull
throat, by the immense length from the ear to the
base of the skull at the back.

I had often seen the Master in life : I had seen
him sipping *absinthe* at the d'Harcourt ; reeling,
a Silenus-like figure, among the nocturnal Bac-
chantes of the Boul' Miche ; lying in the gutter
outside his house, until his mistress should come
to pick him up and take him in. I had seen in the
living man more traces than a few of the bestiality
which the death mask had completely verified ;
but never in the living man had I suspected anything of the beauty, anything of the splendour,
which I now saw.

For that the Master had somewhere a beautiful
soul you divined from his works ; you divined it
from the exquisite melody of all of them, from
the pure, from the ecstatic, from the religious
altitude of some few. But in actual daily life, his
loose and violent will-power, his insane passions,
held that soul bound down so close a captive, that
those who seemed to know him best were the last
to admit its existence.

And here, a mere accident of lighting displayed not only that existence, but its visible, outward expression as well. In these magnificent lines and arches of head and brow, you saw what the man might have been, what God had intended him to be ; what his mother had foreseen in him, when, a tiny infant like Peschi's yonder, she had cradled the warm, downy, sweet-smelling little head upon her bosom, and dreamed day-dreams of all the high, the great, the wonderful things that her boy later on was to do. You saw what the poor, purblind, commonplace mistress was the only one to see, in the seamed and ravaged face she kissed so tenderly for the last time, before the coffin-lid was closed.

You saw the head of gold ; you could forget the feet of clay, or, remembering them, you found in their presence some explanation of the anomalies of his career.

You understood how he who could pour out passionate protestations of love and devotion to God in the morning, offering up body and soul, flesh and blood in His service ; dedicating his brow as a footstool for the Sacred Feet ; his hands as censers for the glowing coals, the precious incense ; condemning his eyes, misleading lights, to be extinguished by the tears of prayer ; you understood how, nevertheless, before evening was come, he would set every law of God and decency at

M

defiance, use every member, every faculty, in the service of sin.

It was given to him, as it is given to few, to see the Best, to reverence it, to love it : and the blind, groping hesitatingly forward in the darkness, do not stray so far as he strayed.

He knew the value of work, its imperative necessity ; that in the sweat of his brow the artist, like the day-labourer, must produce, must produce: and he spent his slothful days shambling from café to café.

He never denied his vices : he recognised them, and found excuses for them, high moral reasons even, as the intellectual man can always do. To indulge them was but to follow out the dictates of Nature, who in herself is holy; cynically to expose them to the world was but to be absolutely sincere.

And his disciples, going further, taught with a vague poetic mysticism that he was a fresh Incarnation of the Godhead; that what was called his immorality was merely his scorn of truckling to the base conventions of the world. But in his saner moments he described himself more accurately as a man blown hither and thither by the winds of evil chance, just as a withered leaf is blown in autumn ; and having received great and exceptional gifts, with Shakespeare's length of years in which to turn them to account, he had

chosen instead to wallow in such vileness that
his very name was anathema among honourable
men.

Chosen ? Did he choose ? Can one say after
all that he chose to resemble the leaf rather than
the tree ? The gates of gifts close on the child
with the womb, and all we possess comes to us
from afar, and is collected from a thousand
diverging sources.

If that splendid head and brow were contained
in the seed, so also were the retreating chin, the
debased jaw, the animal mouth. One as much as
the other was the direct inheritance of former
generations. Considered in a certain aspect, it
seems that a man, by taking thought, may as
little hope to thwart the implanted propensities of
his character, as to alter the shape of his skull or
the size of his jawbone.

I lost myself in mazes of predestination and
free-will. Life appeared to me as a huge kaleido-
scope turned by the hand of Fate. The atoms
of glass coalesce into patterns, fall apart, unite
together again, are always the same, but always
different, and, shake the glass never so slightly,
the precise combination you have just been looking at is broken up for ever. It can never be
repeated. This particular man, with his faults and
his virtues, with his unconscious brutalities, his
unexpected gentlenesses, his furies of remorse ;

this man with the lofty brain, the perverted tastes, the weak, irresolute, indulgent heart, will never again be met to the end of time; in all the endless combinations to come, this precise combination will never be found again. Just as of all the faces the world will see, a face like the mask there will never again exchange glances with it. . . .

I looked at Corner, and saw his countenance once more aglow with the joy of a recovered Ideal; while Peschi's voice broke in on my reverie, speaking with the happy pride of the artist in a good and conscientious piece of work.

"Eh bien, how do you find it ?" said he, "it is beautiful, is it not ?"

THE VILLA LUCIENNE

THE VILLA LUCIENNE

MADAME KOETLEGON told the story, and told it so well that her audience seemed to know the sombre alley, the neglected garden, the shuttered house, as intimately as though they had visited it themselves, seemed to feel a faint reverberation of the incommunicable thrill which she had felt—which the surly guardian, the torn rag of lace, the closed pavilion had made her feel. And yet, as you will see, there is in reality no story at all; it is merely an account of how, when in the Riviera two winters ago, she went with some friends to look over a furnished villa, which one of them thought of taking.

* *
*

It was afternoon when we started on our expedition, Madame de M——, Cécile her widowed daughter-in-law, and I. Cécile's little girl Renée, the nurse, and Médor, the boarhound of which poor Guy had been so inordinately fond, dawdled after us up the steep and sunny road.

The December day was deliciously blue and warm. Cécile took off her furs and carried them over her arm. We only put down our sunshades when a screen of olive-trees on the left interposed their grey-green foliage between us and the sunshine.

Up in these trees barefooted men armed with bamboos were beating the branches to knock down the fruit; and three generations of women, grandmothers, wives, and children, knelt in the grass, gathering up the little purplish olives into baskets. All these paused to follow us with black persistent eyes, as we passed by; but the men went on working unmoved. The tap-tapping, swish-swishing, of their light sticks against the boughs played a characteristically southern accompaniment to our desultory talk.

We were reasonably happy, pleasantly exhilarated by the beauty of the weather and the scene. Renée and Médor, with shrill laughter and deep-mouthed joy-notes, played together the whole way. And when the garden wall, which now replaced the olive-trees upon our right, gave place to a couple of iron gates standing open upon a broad straight drive, and we, looking up between the overarching palm-trees and cocoanuts, saw a white, elegant, sun-bathed house at the end, Cécile jumped to the conclusion that here was the Villa Lucienne, and that nowhere else could she find a house which on the face of it would suit her better.

But the woman who came to greet us, the jocund, brown-faced young woman, with the superb abundance of bosom beneath her crossed neckerchief of orange-coloured wool, told us no; this was the Villa Soleil (appropriate name!) and belonged to Monsieur Morgera, the deputy, who was now in Paris. The Villa Lucienne was higher up; she pointed vaguely behind her through the house; a long walk round by the road. But if these ladies did not mind a path which was a trifle damp perhaps, owing to Monday's rain, they would find themselves in five minutes at the Villa, for the two houses in reality were not more than a stone's throw apart.

She conducted us across a spacious garden golden with sunshine, lyric with bird-song, brilliant with flowers, where eucalyptus, mimosa, and tea-roses interwove their strong and subtle perfumes through the air, to an angle in a remote laurel hedge. Here she stooped to pull aside some ancient pine-boughs which ineffectually closed the entrance to a dark and trellised walk. Peering up it, it seemed to stretch away interminably into green gloom, the ground rising a little all the while, and the steepness of the ascent being modified every here and there by a couple of rotting wooden steps.

We were to go up this alley, our guide told us, and we would be sure to find Laurent at the top. Laurent, she explained to us, was the gardener who lived at the Villa Lucienne and showed it to visitors. But there were not many who came, although it had been to let an immense time, ever since the death of old Madame Gray, and that had occurred before she, the speaker, had come south with the Morgeras. We were to explain to Laurent that we had been sent up from the Villa Soleil, and then it would be all right. For he sometimes used the alley himself, as it gave him a short cut into Antibes ; but the passage had been blocked up many years ago, to prevent the Morgera children running into it.

Oh, Madame was very kind, it was no trouble at all, and of course if these ladies liked they could return by the alley also ; but once they found themselves at the Villa they would be close to the upper road, which they would probably prefer. Then came her cordial voice calling after Cécile, " Madame had best put on her furs again, it is cold in there."

It was cold and damp too, with the damp coldness of places where sun and wind never penetrate. It was so narrow that we had to walk in single file. The walls on either hand, the low roof above our heads, were formed of trellised woodwork dropping into complete decay. But

roof and walls might have been removed altogether,
and the tunnel nevertheless would still have re-
tained its shape; for the creepers which overgrew
it had with time developed gnarled trunks and
branches, which formed a second natural tunnel-
ling outside. Through the broken places in the
woodwork we could see the thick, inextricably
twisted stems ; and beyond again was a tangled
matting of greenery, that suffered no drop of
sunlight to trickle through. The ground was
covered with lichens, deathstools, and a spongy
moss exuding water beneath the foot, and one had
the consciousness that the whole place, floor,
walls, and roof, must creep with the repulsive,
slimy, running life, which pullulates in dark and
solitary places.

The change from the gay and scented garden to
this dull alley, heavy with the smells of moisture
and decay, was curiously depressing. We followed
each other in silence ; first Cécile ; then Renée
clinging to her nurse's hand, with Médor pressing
close against them ; Madame de M—— next ; and
I brought up the rear.

You would have pronounced it impossible to
find in any southern garden so sombre a place,
but that, after all, it is only in the south that such
extraordinary contrasts of gaiety and gloom ever
present themselves.

The sudden tearing away of a portion of one of

the wooden steps beneath my tread startled us all, and the circular scatter of an immense colony of woodlice that had formed its habitat in the crevices of the wood, filled me with shivering disgust. I was exceedingly glad when we emerged from the tunnel upon daylight again and the Villa.

Upon daylight, but not upon sunlight, for the small garden in which we found ourselves was ringed round by the compact tops of the umbrella-pines which climbed the hill on every side. The site had been chosen, of course, on account of the magnificent view which we knew must be obtainable from the Villa windows, though from where we stood we could see nothing but the dark trees, the wild garden, the overshadowed house. And we saw none of these things very distinctly, for our attention was focussed on a man standing there in the middle of the garden, knee-deep in the grass, evidently awaiting us.

He was a short, thick-set peasant, dressed in the immensely wide blue velveteen trousers, the broad crimson sash, and the flannel shirt, open at the throat, which are customary in these parts. He was strong-necked as a bull, dark as a mulatto, and his curling, grizzled hair was thickly matted over head and face and breast. He wore a flat knitted cap, and held the inevitable cigarette between his lips, but he made no attempt to

remove one or the other at our approach. He
stood stolid, silent, his hands thrust deep into
his pockets, staring at us, and shifting from one
to another his suspicious and truculent little
eyes.

So far as I was concerned, and though the Villa
had proved a palace, 1 should have preferred
abandoning the quest at once to going over it in
his company ; but Cécile addressed him with
intrepid politeness.

"We had been permitted to come up from
the Villa Soleil. We understood that the Villa
Lucienne was to let furnished ; if so, might we
look over it ? "

From his heavy, expressionless expression, one
might have supposed that the very last thing he
expected or desired was to find a tenant for the
Villa, and I thought with relief that he was going
to refuse Cécile's request. But, after a longish
pause :

"Yes, you can see it," he said, grudgingly, and
turned from us, to disappear into the lower part
of the house.

We looked into each other's disconcerted faces,
then round the grey and shadowy garden : a
garden long since gone to ruin, with paths and
flower-beds inextricably mingled, with docks and
nettles choking up the rose-trees run wild, with
wind-planted weeds growing from the stone vases

on the terrace, with grasses pushing between the marble steps leading up to the hall door.

In the middle of the lawn a terra-cotta faun, tumbled from his pedestal, grinned sardonically up from amidst the tangled greenery, and Madame de M—— began to quote :

> " Un vieux faune en terre-cuite
> Rit au centre des boulingrins,
> Présageant sans doute une fuite
> De ces instants sereins
> Qui m' ont conduit et t'ont conduite . . ."

The Villa itself was as dilapidated, as mournful-looking as the garden. The ground-floor alone gave signs of occupation, in a checked shirt spread out upon a window-ledge to dry, in a worn besom, an earthenware pipkin, and a pewter jug, ranged against the wall. But the upper part, with the yellow plaster crumbling from the walls, the grey painted persiennes all monotonously closed, said with a thousand voices it was never opened, never entered, had not been lived in for years.

Our surly gardener reappeared, carrying some keys. He led the way up the steps. We exchanged mute questions; all desire to inspect the Villa was gone. But Cécile is a woman of character : she devoted herself.

" I'll just run up and see what it is like," she

said; "it's not worth while you should tire your-self too, Mamma. You, all, wait here."

We stood at the foot of the steps; Laurent was already at the top. Cécile began to mount lightly towards him, but before she was half-way she turned, and to our surprise, "I wish you would come up, all of you," she said, and stopped there until we joined her.

Laurent fitted a key to the door, and it opened with a shriek of rusty hinges. As he followed us, pulling it to behind him, we found ourselves in total darkness. I assure you I went through a bad quarter of a minute. Then we heard the turning of a handle, an inner door was opened, and in the semi-daylight of closed shutters we saw the man's squat figure going from us down a long, old-fashioned, vacant drawing-room towards two windows at the further end.

At the same instant Renée burst into tears:

"Oh, I don't like it. Oh, I'm frightened!" she sobbed.

"Little goosie!" said her grandmother, "see, it's quite light now!" for Laurent had pushed back the persiennes, and a magical panorama had sprung into view: the whole range of the moun-tains behind Nice, their snow-caps suffused with a heavenly rose colour by the setting sun.

But Renée only clutched tighter at Madame de M——'s gown, and wept:

"Oh, I don't like it, Bonnemaman! She is looking at me still. I want to go home!"

"No one is looking at you," her grandmother told her : "talk to your friend Médor. He'll take care of you."

But Renée whispered :

"He wouldn't come in ; he's frightened too."

And, listening, we heard the dog's impatient and complaining bark calling to us from the garden.

Cécile sent Renée and the nurse to join him, and while Laurent let them out, we stepped on to the terrace, and for a moment our hearts were eased by the incomparable beauty of the view, for, raised now above the tree-tops, we looked over the admirable bay, the illimitable sky ; we feasted our eyes upon unimaginable colour, upon matchless form. We were almost prepared to declare that the possession of the Villa was a piece of good fortune not to be let slip, when we heard a step behind us, and turned to see Laurent surveying us morosely from the window threshold, and again to experience the oppression of his ungenial personality.

Under his guidance we now inspected the century-old furniture, the faded silks, the tarnished gilt, the ragged brocades which had once embellished the room. The oval mirrors were dim with mildew, the parquet floor might have been a mere piece of grey drugget, so thick was the overlying

dust.   Curtains, yellowish, ropey, of undetermin-
able material, hung forlornly where once they
had draped windows and doors.   Originally they
may have been of rose satin, for there were traces
of rose colour still on the walls and the ceiling,
painted in gay southern fashion with loves and
doves, festoons of flowers, and knots of ribbons.
But these paintings were all fragmentary, indistinct,
seeming to lose sequence and outline the more
diligently you tried to decipher them.

Yet you could not fail to see that when first
furnished the room must have been charming and
coquettish.   I wondered for whom it had been
thus arranged, why it had been thus abandoned.
For there grew upon me, I cannot tell you why,
the curious conviction that the last inhabitant of
the room having casually left it, had, from some
unexpected obstacle, never again returned.   They
were but the merest trifles that created this idea :
the tiny heap of brown ash which lay on a marble
guéridon, the few withered twigs in the vase
beside it, speaking of the last rose plucked from the
garden ; the big berceuse chair drawn out beside
the sculptured mantelpiece which seemed to retain
the impression of the last occupant ; and in the
dark recesses of the unclosed hearth the smoul-
dering heat which my fancy detected in the half-
charred logs of wood.

The other rooms in the Villa resembled the

N

salon ; each time our surly guide opened the
shutters we saw a repetition of the ancient furniture, of the faded decoration ; everything dust-
covered and time-decayed.   Nor in these other
rooms was any sign of former occupation to be
seen, until, caught upon the girandole of a pier-
glass, a long ragged fragment of lace took my
eye ; an exquisitely fine and cobwebby piece of
lace, as though caught and torn from some gala
shawl or flounce, as the wearer had hurried by.

It was odd perhaps to see this piece of lace
caught thus, but not odd enough surely to account
for the strange emotion which seized hold of me :
an overwhelming pity, succeeded by an overwhelming fear.   I had had a momentary intention
to point the lace out to the others, but a glance at
Laurent froze the words on my lips.   Never in
my life have I experienced such a paralysing fear.
I was filled with an intense desire to get away
from the man and from the Villa.

But Madame de M—— looking from the window, had noticed a pavilion standing isolated in
the garden.   She inquired if it were to be let with
the house.   He gave a surly assent.   Then she
supposed we could visit it.   No, said the man, that
was impossible.   Cécile pointed out it was only
right that tenants should see the whole of the pre-
mises for which they would have to pay, but he
refused this time with so much rudeness, his little

brutish eyes narrowed with so much malignancy, that the panic which I had just experienced now seized the others, and it was a *sauve-qui-peut*.

We gathered up Renée, nurse, and Médor in our hasty passage through the garden, and found our way unguided to the gate upon the upper road.

And once at large beneath the serene evening sky, winding slowly westward down the olive-bordered ways : "What an odious old ruffian !" said one ; "What an eerie, uncanny place !" said another. We compared notes. We found that each of us had been conscious of the same immense, the same inexplicable sense of fear.

Cécile, the least nervous of women, had felt it the first. It had laid hold of her when going up the steps to the door, and it had been so real a terror, she explained to us, that if we had not joined her she would have turned back. Nothing could have induced her to enter the Villa alone.

Madame de M——'s account was that her mind had been more or less troubled from the first moment of entering the garden, but that when the man refused us access to the pavilion, it had been suddenly invaded by a most intolerable sense of wrong. Being very imaginative (poor Guy undoubtedly derived his extraordinary gifts from her), Madame de M—— was convinced that the gardener had murdered some one and buried the body inside the pavilion.

But for me it was not so much the personality of the man—although I admitted he was unprepossessing enough—as the Villa itself which inspired fear. Fear seemed to exude from the walls, to dim the mirrors with its clammy breath, to stir shudderingly among the tattered draperies, to impregnate the whole atmosphere as with an essence, a gas, a contagious disease. You fought it off for a shorter or longer time, according to your powers of resistance, but you were bound to succumb to it at last. The oppressive and invisible fumes had laid hold of us one after the other, and the incident of the closed pavilion had raised our terrors to a ludicrous pitch.

Nurse's experiences, which she gave us a day or two later, supported this view. For she told us that when Renée began to cry, and she took her hand to lead her out, all at once she felt quite nervous and uncomfortable too, as though the little one's trouble had passed by touch into her.

" And what is very strange," said she, " when we reached the garden, there was Médor, his forepaws planted firmly on the ground, his whole body rigid, and his hair bristling all along his backbone from end to end."

Nurse was convinced that both the child and the dog had seen something which we others could not see.

This reminded us of a word of Renée's, a very curious word :

" I don't like it, *she* is looking at me still,"—and Cécile undertook to question her.

" You remember, Renée, when mother took you the other day to look over the pretty Villa——"

Renée opened wide, apprehensive eyes.

" Why did you cry ? "

" I was frightened at the lady," she whispered.

" The lady . . . where was the lady ? " Cécile asked her.

" She was in the drawing-room, sitting in the big chair."

" Was she an old lady like grandmamma, or a young lady like mother ? "

" She was like Bonnemaman," said Renée, and her little mouth began to quiver.

" And what did she do ? "

" She got up and began to—to come——"

But here Renée again burst into tears. And as she is a very nervous, a very excitable child, we had to drop the subject.

But what it all meant, whether there was anything in the history of the house or of its guardian which could account for our sensations, we never knew. We made inquiries, of course, concerning Laurent and the Villa Lucienne, but we learned very little, and that little was so vague, so remote, so irrelevant, that it does not seem worth while repeating.

The indisputable fact is the overwhelming fear which the adventure awoke in each and all of us ; and this effect is impossible to describe, being just the crystallisation of one of those subtle, unformulated emotions in which only poor Guy himself could have hoped to succeed.

SIR JULIAN GARVE

SIR JULIAN GARVE

A YOUNG man, an American, the latest addition
to the hotel colony on the cliff, spent his first
evening as all new-comers invariably do; having
dined, he strolled down the broad, villa-bordered
road, to the Casino on the shore, and went into
the gambling-rooms to look at the play.   He
stopped by the baccarat table.

The sitters were ringed round by a double row
of men, who stood and staked over their shoulders.
But the stranger, on account of his height, could
follow the game easily, and had a good view of
the individual who held the bank.   This was a
man of forty-eight or fifty years of age, handsome,
and even distinguished looking.   Noting his well-
cut clothes, and his imperturbable, his almost
stolid demeanour, the stranger guessed at once
that he was British.   And in spite of the heavy
jaw, of the general stolidity, he was struck by
something fascinating in the man, by something
which suggested to him manifold experiences.

He made these reflections as he idly watched the game. The dealer manipulated the cards with the rapidity and precision of the habitual player. Turning up his own hand he displayed the nine of spades and the ace of diamonds. He helped himself to a third card, and in conformity with an assenting grunt from either side, flung cards to right and left. A murmur arose, half disgust and wholly admiration, for the continued run of luck, which gave the bank, for its third card, the eight of diamonds. The croupier raked together the oblong ivory counters and pushed them over to the Englishman, who swept them into a careless heap and prepared to deal again.

The American, watching, found that his thoughts had travelled to a certain " Professor " Deedes, a professor of conjuring, whose acquaintance he had made at Saratoga during the preceding summer ; an ingenuous, an amusing, a voluble little fellow, who had shown him some surprising tricks with plates and tumblers, with coins and cards. With cards, in particular, the little man had been colossal. In his hands, these remained no mere oblong pieces of pasteboard, but became a troupe of tiny *familiars*, each endowed with a magical knowledge of the Professor's wishes, with an unfailing alacrity in obeying them. One of his tricks had been to take an ordinary pack of fifty-two cards, previously examined and shuffled by the looker-on, and to deal from it nothing but kings and aces ; apparently fifty-two kings and aces. Then fanning out this same pack face downwards, he would invite you to draw a card, and no matter what card you drew, and though you drew many times in succession, invariably this card proved to be—say, the seven of diamonds. He would turn his back while you ran the pack over, making a visual selection ; and the card selected not only divined your choice, but once in the hands of the Professor, found a means of communicating that choice to its master. The young man had been amazed. " But suppose you were to play a game of chance, eh ? " The Professor had replied that he never permitted himself to play games of chance. " Without meaning it, from mere force of habit, I should arrange the cards, I should give myself the game." To demonstrate how safely he could do so, he had dealt as for baccarat, giving himself a total of nine pips every time, and although the young man had been prepared for an exhibition of sleight of hand, although he had been on the look out for it, not to save his life could he have said how it was done.

Now, as he stood watching the play in the Casino, his interest in the game faded before his interest in the problem, as to why at this particular moment, the Saratogan Professor should rise so vividly before his eyes ? It had been a mere twenty-four hours' acquaintanceship, the distraction of a couple of unoccupied afternoons, a thousand succeeding impressions and incidents had superimposed themselves over it since, he had played baccarat a hundred times since, without giving a thought to Deedes. Why then did a picture of the man, of his good humour, his volubility, his unparalleled dexterity, usurp such prominence among his memories at this particular moment ?

.

Preparatory to dealing again, the banker glanced round the table, first at the sitters, then at the circle of men who surrounded them. Here his eye caught the eye of the stranger, and during the brief instant that their glances remained interlocked, the Englishman came to the conclusion that the new-comer had already been observing him for some little time. Then he proceeded with the deal.

When he looked up next he found the stranger occupying the fourth chair to the right, in the place of Morris, the Jew diamond broker, who had gone. Instead of that gentleman's pronounced Hebrew physiognomy, he saw a young face, betraying a dozen races and a million contradictions, with dark hair parted down the middle, hair which had gone prematurely white on top. So that, to the Englishman, with a bit of Herrick run-

ning in his mind, the stranger had the appearance
of having thrust his head into Mab's palace, and
brought away on it all the cobweb tapestries
which adorn her walls.

The young man had a broad and full forehead ;
wore a *pince-nez* which did not conceal the viva-
cious quality of his eyes, and a black beard, short
cut and pointed, which did its best to supplement
his lack of chin.   "Intellectual, witty and humane,
compliant as a woman," commented the Englishman, summing up the stranger's characteristics,
and he was struck with the young man's hands as
he moved them to and fro over the cloth—long-
fingered and finely modelled hands.   He was
struck with their flexibility, with their grace.   He
found himself looking at them with speculation.

"*Faîtes vos jeux, Messieurs,*" cried the voice of
the croupier, and the players pushed their counters over the dividing line.   "*Messieurs, vos jeux
sont faits ?   Rien ne va plus.*"

The bank lost, won, lost again ; seemed in for a
run of ill-luck.   Re-heartened, the players increased their stakes, and Fortune immediately
shifted her wheel, and the croupier's impassive
rake pushed everything on the table over to the
banker.   The young man with the *pince-nez* lost
five hundred marks, a thousand, two thousand, in
succession.   With a steady hand and insouciant
air, he doubled his stake every time, but the bank

continued to win, and the players and bystanders began to look at him with curiosity. He put down five thousand marks and lost them ; he put down ten thousand and saw them raked away.

"Well, that's about cleaned me out," he observed in a casual tone, and got up, to perceive that had he held on for but one more deal he would have recouped all his previous losses. For no sooner had he risen than the bank lost to the side he had just left. His demeanour on receiving this insult at the hands of the jade who had just injured him, if not imperturbable like the Englishman's—and on the contrary, it was all animation —was quite as undecipherable. Not the shrewdest scrutiny could detect whether or no the heart was heavy within, whether the brain which worked behind those astute blue eyes was a prey to anxiety, or in reality as untroubled as those eyes chose to proclaim.

Yet the loss of nearly a thousand pounds would break half the world, and seriously cripple nine-tenths of the remaining half.

The Englishman followed him with thoughtful eyes, as he lighted a cigarette, and with his hands thrust into his trouser pockets, sauntered away into the vestibule.

•

The young man wandered up and down the

marble floor of the vestibule, coaxing his feet to keep straight along a certain line of green marble lozenges which were set at the corners of larger slabs. He amused himself by imagining there was a tremendous precipice on either side of the line, down which the smallest false step would precipitate him. Meanwhile, the man he liked best in the world walked by his side, and endeavoured to draw his attention to more weighty matters.

"There was something crooked about his play, I'll bet you," insinuated this Other. "Why else did you think of the little Professor?"

"Hang it all!" said the young man, carefully keeping his equilibrium, "why shouldn't I think of him? And you see if I could have held on for another turn, I should have won everything back."

"Don't tell me footle like that," came the answer. "Don't tell me that if your money had been lying on the table, the cards would have fallen as they did. But the bank could well afford to lose just then, since the players, intimidated by your losses, had staked so modestly."

The young man arrived safely at the last lozenge, turned, and began the perilous journey back. The Other Fellow turned with him, insisting at his ear: "The man's a card-sharper, a swindler, some poor devil of a half-pay captain, some *chevalier d'industrie* who can't pay his hotel bill."

"You're quite out of it!" returned the young man warmly. "His whole personality refutes you."

"Let's make it a question of character," said the Other Fellow, "and I bet you—well, I bet you twopence that his character won't stand the laxest investigation."

A moment later they both came across Morris. The diamond broker had rendered the young American a small service earlier in the day. His condescension in accepting that service gave him the right now of putting a question.

"Who was the chap holding the bank at the baccarat table?" he asked.

"That was Sir Julian Garve, Bart," said Morris, rolling the words about, as though they were a sweet morsel under the tongue.

"Genuine baronet?"

"As good as they make 'em. Looked him up in Burke. Seats at Knowle and Buckhurst. Arms quarterly or and gules, a bend over all, vert. Though what the devil that means, I'm sure I don't know. Supporters, two leopards, spotted."

"Progenitors of the common garden carriage dog, probably," murmured the young man to his beard. Then, "Hard up?" he queried.

"Looks like it!" answered Morris ironically. "Best rooms at the best hotel in the town, his own cart and blood mares over from England; everything in tip-top style."

"It's very interesting," remarked the young man smiling, and when he smiled his eyelids came together, leaving a mere horizontal gleam of blue.

"Oh, he's very interesting," repeated Morris; "has done a lot, and seen no end."

"I think I should like to know him," observed the young man nonchalantly, and resumed his perigrinations.

⁂

The baccarat party broke up, and Garve, entering the vestibule, arrested Morris in his turn.

"Do you know who it was took your seat at the table this evening?" he inquired.

"Oh, yes; know him well. His name's Underhill. He's an American. Only landed at Hamburg this morning. I happened to be up at the Kronprinz when he arrived, and knowing the ropes there, was able to get him a better room than even the almighty dollar would have procured him."

Garve pondered. "It's to be hoped he's got the almighty dollar in good earnest," said he. "Do you know he's dropped a thousand pounds?"

Morris whistled.

"By-the-bye, has he any one with him?" asked the baronet.

"No, he's quite alone. Come to Europe to study art or literature or some tommy-rot of that sort."

"Then the money was probably his year's screw. I feel very sorry about it."

Morris thought there was no need to fret; evidently he was a millionaire. How else could he afford to waste his time studying art?

But Garve stuck to his own opinion.

"Unless my intuitions are very much at fault," said he, in an impressive undertone, "to-night has struck him a heavy blow. I've known men put an end to themselves for less. You remember poor O'Hagan two seasons back?"

"Oh, yes; but O'Hagan was an emotional Irishman. This chap's not a Yankee for nothing. He's got his head screwed on the right way if ever a man had. Don't think I ever saw a cuter specimen."

Garve looked at the diamond merchant with a tolerant smile. "Of course, being an American, he's necessarily cute, while Irishmen are necessarily emotional, and Englishmen like myself necessarily slow-witted but honest. You allow for no shades in your character-painting. However, I'll try to believe, in this matter, you're right. Look here, he's coming this way now," he added in a moment; "can't you introduce him to me?"

Morris was proud to be in a position to gratify a baronet's wish.

"Allow me to make you and my friend Sir Julian Garve acquainted," said he, as the young man with the *pince-nez* was about to pass them by. "Mr. Francis Underhill, of New York. You'll be surprised at my having got your name and description so pat, but I took the liberty of reading it in the hotel book when I was up there to-day."

The young man removed his glasses, polished them lightly on his silk handkerchief, and readjusted them with care for the purpose of looking the speaker up and down. "Damn his cheek!" the Other Fellow had suggested at his ear.

"No liberty taken by a member of your talented race would ever surprise me, Mr. Moses," he replied.

"My name's Morris," corrected the diamond broker, stiffly.

"Ah, yes, I remember you told me so before; but you see I omitted to impress it on my mind by a reference to the Visitors' Book."

Garve, listening with an air of weary amusement, again caught Underhill's eye, and their glances again interlocked as before at the table. But Garve only said, "I was sorry you had such bad luck to-night." And Underhill thought that the quality of his voice was delightful; it was rich, soft, harmonious. But then, all English voices delighted him.

"Yes," he admitted, "luck was decidedly against me."

Morris alone was unconscious of the dot-long pause which distinguished the word luck.

"To-morrow night you will come and take your revenge," Garve predicted; but there was a note of inquiry in his voice.

"I shall certainly come and play to-morrow," affirmed the young man.

"That's right!" said Garve, cordially. "We shall be glad to see you. We admired your coolness. You're an old hand at the game, evidently."

The attendants were making their presence felt; they were waiting to close the Casino. The three men went out upon the terrace in front, and Garve prepared to take leave.

"You are staying at the Kronprinz, I think?" he said to Underhill. "Then our ways don't lie together, for I always put up in the town. I went there first, long before the cliff hotels were thought of. You came down the upper road, of course? Now, take my advice, and go back by the sands. They're as smooth and firm as a billiard-table, and with this moonlight, you'll have a magnificent walk. Presently you'll come to a zig-zag staircase cut in the cliff, which will bring you up right opposite your hotel."

Underhill and Morris remained some little time longer leaning against the stone balustrade. Above them was a moon-suffused sky, before them a moon-silvered sea. The shrubberies of the Casino gardens sloped down on every side. Over the tops of the foliage on the left glittered the glass dome of the Badeanstaldt, with vacant surrounding sands, which gleamed wetly where the Dürren, dividing into a hundred slender rivulets, flows across them in shallow channels to the sea. Beyond, again, the wooded, widely-curved horn of the bay closed in the western prospect.

Only the extreme tip of the right horn was visible, for immediately to the right of the Casino the land rises abruptly and out-thrusts seawards a bold series of cliffs, crowned from time immemorial by the famous pine forests of Schoenewalder, and, within recent years, by a dozen monster sanatoria and hotels.

Underhill leaned upon the balustrade and looked seawards. He had forgotten his insolence to Morris (he had forgotten Morris's existence), and the Jew had entirely forgiven it. He forgave a good deal in the course of the day to the possessors of rank or wealth. But he was not destitute of good feeling. He was genuinely sorry for the young man, whose silence he attributed to a natural depression on account of his losses. He had a great deal to say next day on the subject of Underhill's low spirits.

When he turned to go, Morris escorted him

through the garden. He wished he could have gone all the way with him, and said so. Terror of Mrs. Morris, whom he knew to be sitting up for him at the Villa Rose, alone prevented him. But this he did not say.

Underhill responded with polite abstraction, and they parted on the crest of the Jew's perfervid hope that they should meet again next day.

The young man sprang lightly down the path which wound to the shore. His first graceless sensation was one of relief that that little bounder had left him. Then, catching sight of the black shadow walking with him over the sands, he made it a courtly salutation.

" For I must confess I'm never in such pleasant company as when I'm alone with you, my dear," he addressed it. The shadow flourished its hat in acknowledgment, and the companions walked on amicably.

" Yet I fancy that fellow Garve could be pleasant company too ! " he threw out tentatively.

" Only it's a pity he cheats at cards, eh ? "

" Bah, bah ! Who says that he cheated ? Isn't it less improbable to believe it was luck than to believe that a man of his position, his wealth, and his appearance—for you'll admit, I suppose, that his appearance is in his favour—is a mere card-sharper, a swindler ? "

"Why, then, did you think of the little Professor?"

"Toujours cette rengaîne!" cried Underhill, with indignation. "What makes me think of the man in the moon at the present moment?"

"Why the moonlight, of course, you blooming duffer!" chuckled his Opponent. "Which establishes my case. Thoughts don't spring up spontaneous in the mind, any more than babies spring up spontaneous under bushes. The kid and the thought are both connected with something which has gone before, although I'll admit that the parentage of both may sometimes be a little difficult to trace. But that gives zest to the pursuit. Now, up on the terrace with Moses, you were thinking that when your year in Europe's over, you'll go home, and ask your delicious little cousin, Annie Laurie, to be your wife."

Underhill broke off to mumur,

> "It was many and many a year ago,
>   In a kingdom by the sea,
> That a maiden there lived, whom you may know
>   By the name of Annabel Lee."

"Oh, stick to business!" urged the Other. "What made you think of Annie?"

"Well, if you really must know," confessed the young man, "I was thinking of my indulgent father and my adoring mother. As Annie Laurie lives with them the connection is obvious."

"And what made you think of your parents ? "

" I was back in God's country."

" How did you get there ? "

" Let me see. . . . . Ah, yes ! I stood on the terrace, looking out over the sea, and observed in the distance the smoke of a steamer. But I don't surely need to follow the thread further, for a person of your intelligence."

" No, but you perceive that you can't possess a thought that hasn't its ancestry lying behind it, any more than you can get from the moonlight here to the shadow there by the cliffs without leaving footprints to show the way you went. Now, when you stood at the baccarat table this evening, what made you think of the little Professor ? "

"My dear chap," said Underhill, "you make me tired. There *is* such a thing as pressing a point too far. And, since you were good enough to call my attention to the fact that the cliff throws a shadow, I'm going to extinguish your Socratic questionings by walking in it. *Buona sera !* "

He rounded a spur of cliff, keeping close to its base.

> " This maiden she had no other thought
>   Than to love and be loved by me;
>   I was a child and she was a child
>   In this kingdom by the sea.
>   But we loved with a love that was more than love,
>   I and my Annabel Lee."

"Now what's the parentage of that quotation?
The similarity of the initials, of course. Oh, my
dear, far be it from me to deny your cleverness !" he concluded gaily, and entered the next
cove.

Across it moved a figure, a real figure, not a
shadow, going from him.   The hands, holding a
light bamboo, were clasped behind the back.

"By Jove, it's Garve !" thought Underhill and
hurried after him.

Garve turned round in surprise.

"I didn't think there was much likelihood of my
overtaking *you*," said he, "but it never occurred
to me you could overtake *me*.   You remained up
at the Casino ?"

"And you didn't go home after all, but put your
advice to me into practice instead ?   Well, it was
good advice too.   The walk is superb.   It's the
sort of night when the thought of bed is a sacri-
lege."

"Even when at home I never go to bed
until daybreak," remarked Garve.   "In civilised
countries, I go on playing until then.   But here,
a grandmotherly government shuts the Casino
at twelve."

"A grandmotherly government knows that
otherwise you wouldn't leave a red cent in the
place," said the young man with a quizzical flash
of blue through his glasses.

Garve stopped to scrutinise him.

"My luck isn't altogether luck perhaps," said he, walking on again.

"No?"

"No," pursued Garve, "it's keeping a cool head, and carefully regulating my life with a view to my play in the evening. I live for cards. I dine at four in the afternoon off roast mutton and rice pudding——"

"Good Lord, how tragic!"

"I go to bed at six and sleep till ten. Then I get up, take a cup of coffee and a biscuit, and come into the rooms with all my wits about me. Naturally, I stand a better chance than the men who've finished off a day of peg-drinking by a heavy indigestible dinner and half-a-dozen different wines."

The young man was amazed, interested, delighted with the absurdity of such an existence.

"As an amusement cards are good enough," said he; "or even at a pinch they might provide the means of livelihood. But why in the world a man of your position should make such sacrifices at their shrine——"

"My position," Garve broke in bitterly, "simply necessitates my spending more money than other men, without furnishing me the wherewithal to do it. I suppose it seems incredible to you Americans, that a man of old family, a man with a handle to his name, shouldn't possess a brass farthing to bless himself with ? "

" Yet I understood from our friend Moses that you had town houses and country houses, manservants and maidservants, oxen and asses, not to mention spotted leopards and blood stock over from England."

The impertinence of this speech was deprived of its sting by the friendly whimsicality of Underhill's manner. Garve accepted it in perfect good part.

" It's just as well Morris and the rest of that crew should think so, but the truth is, I succeeded to an encumbered estate, the rent roll of which barely suffices to pay the mortgage interest. Knowles is let furnished, Buckhurst is so dilapidated no one will hire it. I can't sell, because of the entail. I can't work, for I was never given a profession. I can only play cards; and by playing systematically and regulating, as I tell you, my whole life to that end, I manage to pay my way."

" Twenty thousand dollars in a night," murmured the Other Fellow at Underhill's ear, " would not only pay your way but pave it too. Not ? "

" Oh, dry up ! " advised the young man. " You're such a damned literal chap ! Can't you see he's speaking metaphorically ? "

"So now, you understand the tragedy of the cold mutton," Garve concluded, smiling. They walked on a bit in silence, until Garve resumed in exactly the same even, melodious voice in which he had last spoken, "You thought I cheated to-night, didn't you ?"

Underhill was inexpressibly shocked and pained by this sudden, naked, confrontation with his thought. Besides, he thought it no longer. Garve's explanations had convinced him of Garve's probity ; he was subjugated by Garve's charm.

"No, no, no ! Don't say such things !" he protested. "A thousand times no !"

"All the same, you thought I cheated," repeated Garve standing still, and looking at him oddly. "And—— I did cheat ! . . . I lost only when it suited my purpose to lose. Every time I had forced the cards."

He remained imperturbable, cold, as he said this. It was, perhaps, only the moonlight that made his handsome face look haggard and pale.

On the other hand, it was the young American who coloured up to the roots of his hair, who was overcome with horror, who was conscious of all the shame, of all the confusion which the confessed swindler might be supposed to feel. And when Garve sat on a boulder, and covered his ace with his hand, Underhill longed to sink through the earth, that he might not witness his humiliation.

He tried to say something comforting. The words would not form themselves, or stumbled out disjointedly, irrelevantly.

Garve did not listen.

"I've lost the last thing I had in the world to lose," said he ; "my honour. I carry a besmirched name. I am a ruined, a broken man. You found me out to-night. Even if you spare me, another will find me out another night. And how to live with the knowledge that you know my shame ! How to live ! How to live !"

He got up. His stick lay on the sand. He took a few uncertain steps with bowed head, and his hand thrust into his breast. He came back to where the young man stood.

"There's but one thing left for me to do," said he, looking at him with sombre eyes, " and that's to shoot myself. Don't you see yourself it's all that remains for me to do ? "

Underhill's quick brain envisaged the man's whole life, the infamy of it, the pathos of it. He recognised the impossibility of living down such a past, he foresaw the degrading years to come. He knew that Garve had found the only solution possible. He knew it was what he himself would do in the same hideous circumstances. Yet how could he counsel this other to do it ? This other for whom his heart was wrung, for whom he felt warm sympathy, compassion, brotherliness. Oh, there must be some other way !

While he hesitated, while he searched for it, Garve repeated his proposition. "There's only one thing for me to do, shoot myself, eh ? Or," he paused . . . " shoot the man who's found me out ? I might, for instance, shoot you ? "

Underhill was conscious of a smart blow on the ear. He started back looking at Garve with surprise. For the fraction of a second he thought Garve had really shot him . . . but that was absurd . . . a little blow like that ! Yet what then did he mean by it ? Garve stood staring across at him, staring, staring, and between the fingers of his right hand, which was falling back to his side, was a glint of steel. Motionless in air between the two men hung a tiny swirl of smoke.

" Is it possible ? is it possible ? " Underhill asked himself. And all at once Garve seemed to be removed an immense way off ; he saw him blurred, wavering, indistinct. Then it was no longer Garve, it was his father, over whose shoulder appeared his mother's face, and Annie Laurie's. . . . He tried to spring to them, but his legs refused to obey him. He dropped to his knees instead, and all thought and all sensation suddenly ceased . . .

The body sank over into the sand.

Printed by BALLANTYNE, HANSON & Co.
London & Edinburgh

List of Books

IN

BELLES LETTRES

Published by John Lane

ᵗᵍᵉ ᵍᵒᵈᶅᵉᵖ ᵍᵉᵃᵈ

VIGO STREET, LONDON, W.

Adams (Francis).
ESSAYS IN MODERNITY. Crown 8vo.
5s. net.   [*Shortly.*
A CHILD OF THE AGE. Crown 8vo.
3s. 6d. net.

A. E.
HOMEWARD: SONGS BY THE WAY.
Sq. 16mo, wrappers, 1s. 6d. net.
                    [*Second Edition.*
THE EARTH BREATH, AND OTHER
POEMS. Sq. 16mo. 3s. 6d. net.

Aldrich (T. B.).
LATER LYRICS. Sm. fcap. 8vo.
2s. 6d. net.

Allen (Grant).
THE LOWER SLOPES : A Volume of
Verse. Crown 8vo. 5s. net.
THE WOMAN WHO DID. Crown
8vo. 3s. 6d. net.
                    [*Twenty-third Edition.*
THE BRITISH BARBARIANS. Crown
8vo. 3s. 6d. net.
                    [*Second Edition.*

Atherton (Gertrude).
PATIENCE SPARHAWK AND HER
TIMES. Crown 8vo. 6s.
                    [*Third Edition*
THE CALIFORNIANS. Crown 8vo.
6s.   [*Shortly.*

Bailey (John C.).
ENGLISH ELEGIES. Crown 8vo.
5s. net.   [*In preparation.*

Balfour (Marie Clothilde).
MARIS STELLA. Crown 8vo. 3s. 6d.
net.
SONGS FROM A CORNER OF FRANCE.
                    [*In preparation.*

Beeching (Rev. H. C.).
IN A GARDEN : Poems. Crown 8vo.
5s. net.
ST. AUGUSTINE AT OSTIA. Crown
8vo, wrappers. 1s. net.

Beerbohm (Max).
THE WORKS OF MAX BEERBOHM.
With a Bibliography by JOHN
LANE. Sq. 16mo. 4s. 6d. net.
THE HAPPY HYPOCRITE. Sq. 16mo.
1s. net.   [*Third Edition.*

Bennett (E. A.).
A MAN FROM THE NORTH.
Crown 8vo. 3s. 6d.
JOURNALISM FOR WOMEN: A Prac-
tical Guide. Sq. 16mo. 2s. 6d. net.

**Benson (Arthur Christo-
pher).**
LYRICS. Fcap. 8vo, buckram. 5s.
net.
LORD VYET AND OTHER POEMS.
Fcap. 8vo. 3s. 6d. net.

Bridges (Robert).
SUPPRESSED CHAPTERS AND OTHER
BOOKISHNESS. Crown 8vo. 3s. 6d.
net.   [*Second Edition.*

Brotherton (Mary).
ROSEMARY FOR REMEMBRANCE.
Fcap. 8vo. 3s. 6d. net.

Brown (Vincent).
MY BROTHER. Sq. 16mo. 2s. net.
ORDEAL BY COMPASSION. Crown
8vo. 3s. 6d.
TWO IN CAPTIVITY. Crown 8vo.
3s. 6d.   [*In preparation.*

Bourne (George).
A YEAR'S EXILE. Crown 8vo.
3s. 6d.

Buchan (John).
SCHOLAR GIPSIES. With 7 full-page Etchings by D. Y. CAMERON. Crown 8vo. 5s. net.
[*Second Edition.*
MUSA PISCATRIX. With 6 Etchings by E. PHILIP PIMLOTT. Crown 8vo. 5s. net.
GREY WEATHER. Crown 8vo. 5s. [*In preparation,*
JOHN BURNET OF BARNS. A Romance. Crown 8vo. 6s.

Campbell (Gerald).
THE JONESES AND THE ASTERISKS. A Story in Monologue. 6 Illustrations by F. H. TOWNSEND. Fcap. 8vo. 3s. 6d. net.
[*Second Edition.*

Case (Robert H.).
ENGLISH EPITHALAMIES. Crown 8vo. 5s. net.

Castle (Mrs. Egerton).
MY LITTLE LADY ANNE. Sq. 16mo. 2s. net.

Chapman(ElizabethRachel)
MARRIAGE QUESTIONS IN MODERN FICTION. Crown 8vo. 3s. 6d. net.

Charles (Joseph F.).
THE DUKE OF LINDEN. Crown 8vo. 5s. [*In preparation.*

Cobb (Thomas).
CARPET COURTSHIP. Crown 8vo. 3s. 6d.
MR. PASSINGHAM. Crown 8vo. 3s. 6d. [*In preparation.*

Coleridge (Ernest Hartley).
POEMS. 3s. 6d. net.

Corvo (Baron).
STORIES TOTO TOLD ME. Square 16mo. 1s. net.

Crane (Walter).
TOY BOOKS. Re-issue of.
This LITTLE PIG'S PICTURE BOOK, containing:
I. THIS LITTLE PIG.
II. THE FAIRY SHIP.
III. KING LUCKIEBOY'S PARTY.
MOTHER HUBBARD'S PICTURE-BOOK, containing:
IV. MOTHER HUBBARD.
V. THE THREE BEARS.
VI. THE ABSURD A. B. C.

Crane (Walter)—*continued.*
CINDERELLA'S PICTURE BOOK, containing:
VII. CINDERELLA.
VIII. PUSS IN BOOTS.
IX. VALENTINE AND ORSON.
Each Picture-Book containing three Toy Books, complete with end papers and covers, together with collective titles, end-papers, decorative cloth cover, and newly written Preface by WALTER CRANE, 4s. 6d. The Nine Parts as above may be had separately at 1s. each.

Crackanthorpe (Hubert).
VIGNETTES. A Miniature Journal of Whim and Sentiment. Fcap. 8vo, boards. 2s. 6d. net.

Craig (R. Manifold).
THE SACRIFICE OF FOOLS. Crown 8vo. 6s.

Crosse (Victoria).
THE WOMAN WHO DIDN'T. Crown 8vo. 3s. 6d. net.
[*Third Edition.*

Custance (Olive).
OPALS: Poems. Fcap. 8vo. 3s. 6d. net.

Croskey (Julian).
MAX. Crown 8vo. 6s.
[*Second Edition.*

Dalmon (C. W.).
SONG FAVOURS. Sq. 16mo. 3s. 6d. net.

D'Arcy (Ella).
MONOCHROMES. Crown 8vo. 3s. 6d. net.
THE BISHOP'S DILEMMA. Crown 8vo. 3s. 6d.
MODERN INSTANCES. Crown 8vo. 3s. 6d.

Dawe (W. Carlton).
YELLOW AND WHITE. Crown 8vo. 3s. 6d. net.
KAKEMONOS. Crown 8vo. 3s. 6d. net.

Dawson (A. J.)
MERE SENTIMENT. Crown 8vo. 3s. 6d. net.
MIDDLE GREYNESS. Crown 8vo. 6s.

Davidson (John).
PLAYS: An Unhistorical Pastoral; A Romantic Farce; Bruce, a Chronicle Play; Smith, a Tragic Farce; Scaramouch in Naxos, a Pantomime. Small 4to. 7s. 6d. net.

Davidson (John)—_continued._
FLEET STREET ECLOGUES. Fcap.
8vo, buckram. 4s. 6d. net.
[_Third Edition._
FLEET STREET ECLOGUES. 2nd
Series. Fcap. 8vo, buckram.
4s. 6d. net. [_Second Edition._
A RANDOM ITINERARY. Fcap. 8vo.
5s. net.
BALLADS AND SONGS. Fcap. 8vo.
5s. net. [_Fourth Edition._
NEW BALLADS. Fcap. 8vo. 4s. 6d.
net. [_Second Edition._
GODFRIDA. A Play. Fcap. 3vo. 5s.
net.

De Lyrienne (Richard).
THE QUEST OF THE GILT-EDGED
GIRL. Sq. 16mo. 1s. net.

De Tabley (Lord).
POEMS, DRAMATIC AND LYRICAL.
By JOHN LEICESTER WARREN
(Lord de Tabley). Five Illus-
trations and Cover by C. S.
RICKETTS. Crown 8vo. 7s. 6d.
net. [_Third Edition._
POEMS, DRAMATIC AND LYRICAL.
Second Series. Crown 8vo. 5s. net.

Devereux (Roy).
THE ASCENT OF WOMAN. Crown
8vo. 3s. 6d. net.

Dick (Chas. Hill).
ENGLISH SATIRES. Crown 8vo. 5s.
net. [_In preparation._

Dix (Gertrude).
THE GIRL FROM THE FARM. Crown
8vo. 3s. 6d. net. [_Second Edition._

Dostoievsky (F.).
POOR FOLK. Translated from the
Russian by LENA MILMAN. With
a Preface by GEORGE MOORE.
Crown 8vo. 3s. 6d. net.

Dowie (Menie Muriel).
SOME WHIMS OF FATE. Post 8vo.
2s. 6d. net.

Duer (Caroline, and Alice).
POEMS. Fcap. 8vo. 3s. 6d. net.

Egerton (George).
KEYNOTES. Crown 8vo. 3s. 6d. net.
[_Eighth Edition._
DISCORDS. Crown 8vo. 3s. 6d. net.
[_Fifth Edition._
SYMPHONIES. Crown 8vo. 6s.
[_Second Edition._
FANTASIAS. Crown 8vo. 3s. 6d.
THE HAZARD OF THE ILL. Crown
8vo. 6s. [_In preparation._

Eglinton (John).
TWO ESSAYS ON THE REMNANT.
Post 8vo, wrappers. 1s. 6d. net.
[_Second Edition._

Farr (Florence).
THE DANCING FAUN. Crown 8vo.
3s. 6d. net.

Fea (Allan).
THE FLIGHT OF THE KING : A full,
true, and particular account of the
escape of His Most Sacred Ma-
jesty King Charles II. after the
Battle of Worcester, with Sixteen
Portraits in Photogravure and
over 100 other Illustrations. Demy
8vo. 21s. net.

Field (Eugene).
THE LOVE AFFAIRS OF A BIBLIO-
MANIAC. Post 8vo. 3s. 6d. net.
LULLABY LAND : Songs of Child-
hood. Edited, with Introduction,
by KENNETH GRAHAME. With 200
Illustrations by CHAS. ROBINSON.
Uncut or gilt edges. Crown 8vo. 6s.

Firth (George).
THE ADVENTURES OF A MARTYR'S
BIBLE. Crown 8vo. 6s.

Fleming (George).
FOR PLAIN WOMEN ONLY. Fcap.
8vo. 3s. 6d. net.

Flowerdew (Herbert).
A CELIBATE'S WIFE. Crown 8vo.
6s.

Fletcher (J. S.).
THE WONDERFUL WAPENTAKE.
By "A SON OF THE SOIL." With
18 Full-page Illustrations by J. A.
SYMINGTON. Crown 8vo. 5s. 6d.
net.
LIFE IN ARCADIA. With 20 Illustrations by PATTEN WILSON. Crown
8vo. 5s. net.
GOD'S FAILURES. Crown 8vo. 3s. 6d.
net.
BALLADS OF REVOLT. Sq. 32mo.
2s. 6d. net.
THE MAKING OF MATTHIAS. With
40 Illustrations and Decorations
by LUCY KEMP-WELCH. Crown
8vo. 5s.

Ford (James L.).
THE LITERARY SHOP, AND OTHER
TALES. Fcap. 8vo. 3s. 6d. net.

Frederic (Harold).
MARCH HARES. Crown 8vo. 3s. 6d. net. [Third Edition.
MRS. ALBERT GRUNDY: OBSERVATIONS IN PHILISTIA. Fcap. 8vo. 3s. 6d. net. [Second Edition.

Fuller (H. B.).
THE PUPPET BOOTH. Twelve Plays. Crown 8vo. 4s. 6d. net.

Gale (Norman).
ORCHARD SONGS. Fcap. 8vo. 5s. net.

Garnett (Richard).
POEMS. Crown 8vo. 5s. net.
DANTE, PETRARCH, CAMOENS, cxxiv Sonnets, rendered in English. Crown 8vo. 5s. net.

Geary (Sir Nevill).
A LAWYER'S WIFE. Crown 8vo. 6s. [Second Edition.

Gibson (Charles Dana).
DRAWINGS: Eighty-Five Large Cartoons. Oblong Folio. 20s.
PICTURES OF PEOPLE. Eighty-Five Large Cartoons. Oblong folio. 20s.
LONDON: AS SEEN BY C. D. GIBSON. Text and Illustrations. Large folio, 12 × 18 inches. 20s.
THE PEOPLE OF DICKENS. Six Large Photogravures. Proof Impressions from Plates, in a Portfolio. 20s.

Gilbert (Henry).
OF NECESSITY. Crown 8vo. 3s. 6d.

Gilliat-Smith (E.)
SONGS FROM PRUDENTIUS. Pott 4to. 5s. net.

Gleig (Charles)
WHEN ALL MEN STARVE. Crown 8vo. 3s. 6d.
THE EDGE OF HONESTY. Crown 8vo. 6s.

Gosse (Edmund).
THE LETTERS OF THOMAS LOVELL BEDDOES. Now first edited. Pott 8vo. 5s. net.

Grahame (Kenneth).
PAGAN PAPERS. Crown 8vo. 3s. 6d. net. [Second Edition.
THE GOLDEN AGE. Crown 8vo. 3s. 6d. net. [Eighth Edition.
A NEW VOLUME OF ESSAYS. [In preparation.
See EUGENE FIELD'S LULLABY LAND.

Greene (G. A.).
ITALIAN LYRISTS OF TO-DAY. Translations in the original metres from about thirty-five living Italian poets, with bibliographical and biographical notes. Crown 8vo. 5s. net. [Second Edition.

Greenwood (Frederick).
IMAGINATION IN DREAMS. Crown 8vo. 5s. net.

Grimshaw (Beatrice Ethel).
BROKEN AWAY. Crown 8vo. 3s. 6d. net.

Hake (T. Gordon).
A SELECTION FROM HIS POEMS. Edited by Mrs. MEYNELL. With a Portrait after D. G. ROSSETTI. Crown 8vo. 5s. net.

Hansson (Laura M.).
MODERN WOMEN. An English rendering of "DAS BUCH DER FRAUEN" by HERMIONE RAMSDEN. Subjects: Sonia Kovalevsky, George Egerton, Eleanora Duse, Amalie Skram, Marie Bashkirtseff, A. Ch. Edgren Leffler. Crown 8vo. 3s. 6d. net.

Hansson (Ola).
YOUNG OFEG'S DITTIES. A Translation from the Swedish. By GEORGE EGERTON. Crown 8vo. 3s. 6d. net.

Harland (Henry).
GREY ROSES. Crown 8vo, 3s. 6d. net.
COMEDIES AND ERRORS. Crown 8vo. 6s.

Hay (Colonel John).
POEMS INCLUDING "THE PIKE COUNTY BALLADS" (Author's Edition), with Portrait of the Author. Crown 8vo. 4s. 6d. net.
CASTILIAN DAYS. Crown 8vo. 4s. 6d. net.
SPEECH AT THE UNVEILING OF THE BUST OF SIR WALTER SCOTT IN WESTMINSTER ABBEY. With a Drawing of the Bust. Sq. 16mo. 1s. net.

Hayes (Alfred).
THE VALE OF ARDEN AND OTHER POEMS. Fcap. 8vo. 3s. 6d. net.

Hazlitt (William).

LIBER AMORIS; OR, THE NEW
PYGMALION. Edited, with an
Introduction, by RICHARD LE
GALLIENNE. To which is added an
exact transcript of the original MS.,
Mrs. Hazlitt's Diary in Scotland,
and letters never before published.
Portrait after BEWICK, and fac-
simile letters. 400 Copies only. 4to,
364 pp., buckram. 21s. net.

Heinemann (William).

THE FIRST STEP; A Dramatic
Moment. Small 4to. 3s. 6d. net.
SUMMER MOTHS: A Play. Sm.
4to. 3s. 6d. net.

Henniker (Florence).

IN SCARLET AND GREY. (With
THE SPECTRE OF THE REAL by
FLORENCE HENNIKER and
THOMAS HARDY.) Crown 8vo.
3s. 6d. net. [Second Edition.

Hickson (Mrs. Murray).

SHADOWS OF LIFE. Crown 8vo.
3s. 6d.

Hopper (Nora).

BALLADS IN PROSE. Sm. 4to. 6s.
UNDER QUICKEN BOUGHS. Crown
8vo. 5s. net.

Housman (Clemence).

THE WERE WOLF. With 6 Illustrations by LAURENCE HOUSMAN.
Sq. 16mo. 3s. 6d. net.

Housman (Laurence).

GREEN ARRAS: Poems. With 6
Illustrations, Title-page, Cover
Design, and End Papers by the
Author. Crown 8vo. 5s. net.
GODS AND THEIR MAKERS. Crown
8vo, 3s. 6d. net.

Irving (Laurence).

GODEFROI AND YOLANDE: A Play.
Sm. 4to. 3s. 6d. net.

Jalland (G. H.).

THE SPORTING ADVENTURES OF
MR. POPPLE. Coloured Plates.
Oblong 4to, 14 × 10 inches. 6s.
[In preparation.

James (W. P.)

ROMANTIC PROFESSIONS: A Volume
of Essays. Crown 8vo. 5s. net.

Johnson (Lionel).

THE ART OF THOMAS HARDY: Six
Essays. With Etched Portrait by
WM. STRANG, and Bibliography
by JOHN LANE. Crown 8vo.
5s. 6d. net. [Second Edition.

Johnson (Pauline).

WHITE WAMPUM : Poems. Crown
8vo. 5s. net.

Johnstone (C. E.).

BALLADS OF BOY AND BEAK. Sq.
32mo. 2s. net.

Kemble (E. W.)

KEMBLE'S COONS. 30 Drawings of
Coloured Children and Southern
Scenes. Oblong 4to. 6s.

King (K. Douglas).

THE CHILD WHO WILL NEVER GROW
OLD. Crown 8vo. 5s.

King (Maud Egerton).

ROUND ABOUT A BRIGHTON COACH
OFFICE. With over 30 Illustra-
tions by LUCY KEMP-WELCH.
Crown 8vo. 5s. net.

Lander (Harry).

WEIGHED IN THE BALANCE.
Crown 8vo. 6s.

The Lark.

BOOK THE FIRST. Containing
Nos. 1 to 12.
BOOK THE SECOND. Containing
Nos. 13 to 24. With numerous
Illustrations by GELETT BURGESS
and Others. Small 4to. 25s. net.
the set. [All published.

Leather (R. K.).

VERSES. 250 copies. Fcap. 8vo.
5s. net.

Lefroy (Edward Cracroft).

POEMS. With a Memoir by W. A.
GILL, and a reprint of Mr. J. A.
SYMONDS' Critical Essay on
"Echoes from Theocritus." Cr.
8vo. Photogravure Portrait. 5s.
net.

Le Gallienne (Richard).

PROSE FANCIES. With Portrait of
the Author by WILSON STEER.
Crown 8vo. 5s. net.
[Fourth Edition.
THE BOOK BILLS OF NARCISSUS.
An Account rendered by RICHARD
LE GALLIENNE. With a Frontis-
piece. Crown 8vo. 3s. 6d. net.
[Third Edition.

Le Gallienne (Richard)—
continued.
ROBERT LOUIS STEVENSON, AN ELEGY, AND OTHER POEMS, MAINLY PERSONAL. Crown 8vo. 4s. 6d. net.
ENGLISH POEMS. Crown 8vo. 4s. 6d. net.
[*Fourth Edition, revised.*
GEORGE MEREDITH: Some Characteristics. With a Bibliography (much enlarged) by JOHN LANE, portrait, &c. Crown 8vo. 5s. 6d. net.   [*Fourth Edition.*
THE RELIGION OF A LITERARY MAN. Crown 8vo. 3s. 6d. net.
[*Fifth Thousand.*
RETROSPECTIVE REVIEWS, A LITERARY LOG, 1891-1895. 2 vols. Crown 8vo. 9s. net.
PROSE FANCIES. (Second Series). Crown 8vo. 5s. net.
THE QUEST OF THE GOLDEN GIRL. Crown 8vo. 6s. [*Fifth Edition.*
THE ROMANCE OF ZION CHAPEL. Crown 8vo. 6s.
LOVE IN LONDON: Poems. Crown 8vo. 4s. 6d. net. [*In preparation.*
See also HAZLITT, WALTON and COTTON.

Legge (A. E. J.).
MUTINEERS. Crown 8vo. 6s.

Linden (Annie).
GOLD. A Dutch Indian story. Crown 8vo. 3s. 6d. net.

Lipsett (Caldwell).
WHERE THE ATLANTIC MEETS THE LAND. Crown 8vo. 3s. 6d. net.

Locke (W. J.).
DERELICTS. Crown 8vo. 6s.
[*Second Edition.*

Lowry (H. D.).
MAKE BELIEVE. Illustrated by CHARLES ROBINSON. Crown 8vo, gilt edges or uncut. 6s.
WOMEN'S TRAGEDIES. Crown 8vo. 3s. 6d. net.
THE HAPPY EXILE. With 6 Etchings by E. PHILIP PIMLOTT. Crown 8vo. 6s.

Lucas (Winifred).
UNITS: Poems. Fcap. 8vo. 3s. 6d. net.

Lynch (Hannah).
THE GREAT GALEOTO AND FOLLY OR SAINTLINESS. Two Plays, from the Spanish of JOSÉ ECHEGARAY, with an Introduction. Small 4to. 5s. 6d. net.

McChesney (Dora Greenwell).
BEATRIX INFELIX. A Summer Tragedy in Rome. Crown 8vo. 3s. 6d.

Macgregor (Barrington).
KING LONGBEARD. With over 100 Illustrations by CHARLES ROBINSON. Small 4to. 6s.

Machen (Arthur).
THE GREAT GOD PAN AND THE INMOST LIGHT. Crown 8vo. 3s. 6d. net.   [*Second Edition.*
THE THREE IMPOSTORS. Crown 8vo. 3s. 6d. net.

Macleod (Fiona).
THE MOUNTAIN LOVERS. Crown 8vo. 3s. 6d. net.

Makower (Stanley V.).
THE MIRROR OF MUSIC. Crown 8vo. 3s. 6d. net.
CECILIA. Crown 8vo. 5s.

Mangan (James Clarence).
SELECTED POEMS. With a Biographical and Critical Preface by LOUISE IMOGEN GUINEY. Crown 8vo. 5s. net.

Mathew (Frank).
THE WOOD OF THE BRAMBLES. Crown 8vo. 6s.
A CHILD IN THE TEMPLE. Crown 8vo. 3s. 6d.
THE SPANISH WINE. Crown 8vo. 3s. 6d.
AT THE RISING OF THE MOON. Crown 8vo. 3s. 6d.

Marzials (Theo.).
THE GALLERY OF PIGEONS AND OTHER POEMS. Post 8vo. 4s. 6d. net.

Meredith (George).
THE FIRST PUBLISHED PORTRAIT OF THIS AUTHOR, engraved on the wood by W. BISCOMBE GARDNER, after the painting by G. F. WATTS. Proof copies on Japanese vellum, signed by painter and engraver. £1 1s. net.

Meynell (Mrs.).

POEMS. Fcap. 8vo. 3s. 6d. net.
[Sixth Edition.

THE RHYTHM OF LIFE AND OTHER
ESSAYS. Fcap. 8vo. 3s. 6d. net.
[Sixth Edition.

THE COLOUR OF LIFE AND OTHER
ESSAYS. Fcap. 8vo. 3s. 6d.
net. [Fifth Edition.

THE CHILDREN. Fcap. 8vo. 3s. 6d.
net. [Second Edition.

Miller (Joaquin).

THE BUILDING OF THE CITY BEAU-
TIFUL. Fcap. 8vo. With a
Decorated Cover. 5s. net.

Milman (Helen).

IN THE GARDEN OF PEACE. With
24 Illustrations by EDMUND H.
NEW. Crown 8vo. 5s. net.
[Second Edition.

Money-Coutts (F. B.).

POEMS. Crown 8vo. 3s. 6d. net.

THE REVELATION OF ST. LOVE THE
DIVINE. Sq. 16mo. 3s. 6d. net.

Monkhouse (Allan).

BOOKS AND PLAYS: A Volume of
Essays on Meredith, Borrow,
Ibsen, and others. Crown 8vo.
5s. net.

A DELIVERANCE. Crown 8vo.
5s. [In preparation.

Nesbit (E.).

A POMANDER OF VERSE. Crown
8vo. 5s. net.

IN HOMESPUN. Crown 8vo. 3s. 6d.
net.

Nettleship (J. T.).

ROBERT BROWNING: Essays and
Thoughts. Portrait. Crown 8vo.
5s. 6d. net. [Third Edition.

Nicholson (Claud).

UGLY IDOL. Crown 8vo. 3s. 6d.
net.

Noble (Jas. Ashcroft).

THE SONNET IN ENGLAND AND
OTHER ESSAYS. Crown 8vo. 5s.
net.

Oppenheim (M.).

A HISTORY OF THE ADMINISTRA-
TION OF THE ROYAL NAVY, and
of Merchant Shipping in relation
to the Navy from MDIX to
MDCLX, with an introduction
treating of the earlier period. With
Illustrations. Demy 8vo. 15s.
net.

Orred (Meta).

GLAMOUR. Crown 8vo. 6s.

O'Shaughnessy (Arthur).

HIS LIFE AND HIS WORK. With
Selections from his Poems. By
LOUISE CHANDLER MOULTON.
Portrait and Cover Design. Fcap.
8vo. 5s. net.

Oxford Characters.

A series of lithographed portraits by
WILL ROTHENSTEIN, with text
by F. YORK POWELL and others.
200 copies only, folio. £3 3s.
net.

Pain (Barry).

THE TOMPKINS VERSES. Edited
by BARRY PAIN, with an introduction. Crown 8vo. 3s. 6d.
[In preparation.

Pennell (Elizabeth Robins).

THE FEASTS OF AUTOLYCUS: THE
DIARY OF A GREEDY WOMAN.
Fcap. 8vo. 3s. 6d. net.

Peters (Wm. Theodore).

POSIES OUT OF RINGS. Sq. 16mo.
2s. 6d. net.

Phillips (Stephen).

POEMS. With which is incor-
porated "CHRIST IN HADES."
Crown 8vo. 4s. 6d. net.
[Fourth Edition.

Pinkerton (T. A.).

SUN BEETLES. Crown 8vo. 3s. 6d.

Plarr (Victor).

IN THE DORIAN MOOD: Poems
Crown 8vo. 5s. net.

Posters in Miniature: over
250 reproductions of French,
English and American Posters,
with Introduction by EDWARD
PENFIELD. Large crown 8vo.
5s. net.

Price (A. T. G.).

SIMPLICITY. Sq. 16mo. 2s. net.

Radford (Dollie).

SONGS AND OTHER VERSES. Fcap.
8vo. 4s. 6d. net.

Risley (R. V.).

THE SENTIMENTAL VIKINGS. Post
8vo. 2s. 6d. net.

Rhys (Ernest).

A LONDON ROSE AND OTHER
RHYMES. Crown 8vo. 5s. net.

Robertson (John M.).
NEW ESSAYS TOWARDS A CRITICAL METHOD. Crown 8vo. 6s. net.

Russell (T. Baron).
A GUARDIAN OF THE POOR. Crown 8vo. 3s. 6d.

St. Cyres (Lord).
THE LITTLE FLOWERS OF ST. FRANCIS: A new rendering into English of the Fioretti di San Francesco. Crown 8vo. 5s. net. [In preparation.

Seaman (Owen).
THE BATTLE OF THE BAYS. Fcap. 8vo. 3s. 6d. net. [Fourth Edition.
HORACE AT CAMBRIDGE. Crown 8vo. 3s. 6d. net.

Sedgwick (Jane Minot).
SONGS FROM THE GREEK. Fcap. 8vo. 3s. 6d. net.

Setoun (Gabriel).
THE CHILD WORLD : Poems. With over 200 Illustrations by CHARLES ROBINSON. Crown 8vo, gilt edges or uncut. 6s.

Sharp (Evelyn).
WYMPS : Fairy Tales. With 8 Coloured Illustrations by Mrs. PERCY DEARMER. Small 4to, decorated cover. 6s. [Second Edition.
AT THE RELTON ARMS. Crown 8vo. 3s. 6d. net.
THE MAKING OF A PRIG. Crown 8vo. 6s.
ALL THE WAY TO FAIRY LAND. With 8 Coloured Illustrations by Mrs. PERCY DEARMER. Small 4to, decorated cover. 6s. [Second Edition.

Shiel (M. P.).
PRINCE ZALESKI. Crown 8vo. 3s. 6d. net.
SHAPES IN THE FIRE. Crown 8vo. 3s. 6d. net.

Shore (Louisa).
POEMS. With an appreciation by FREDERIC HARRISON and a Portrait. Fcap. 8vo. 5s. net.

Shorter (Mrs. Clement) (Dora Sigerson).
THE FAIRY CHANGELING, AND OTHER POEMS. Crown 8vo. 3s. 6d. net.

Smith (John).
PLATONIC AFFECTIONS. Crown 8vo. 3s. 6d. net.

Stacpoole (H. de Vere).
PIERROT. Sq. 16mo. 2s. net.
DEATH, THE KNIGHT, AND THE LADY. Crown 8vo. 3s. 6d.

Stevenson (Robert Louis).
PRINCE OTTO. A Rendering in French by EGERTON CASTLE. Crown 8vo. 7s. 6d. net.
A CHILD'S GARDEN OF VERSES. With over 150 Illustrations by CHARLES ROBINSON. Crown 8vo. 5s. net. [Fourth Edition.

Stimson (F. J.).
KING NOANETT. A Romance of Devonshire Settlers in New England. With 12 Illustrations by HENRY SANDHAM. Crown 8vo. 6s.

Stoddart (Thos. Tod).
THE DEATH WAKE. With an Introduction by ANDREW LANG. Fcap. 8vo. 5s. net.

Street (G. S.).
EPISODES. Post 8vo. 3s. net.
MINIATURES AND MOODS. Fcap. 8vo. 3s. net.
QUALES EGO : A FEW REMARKS, IN PARTICULAR AND AT LARGE. Fcap. 8vo. 3s. 6d. net.
THE AUTOBIOGRAPHY OF A BOY. Fcap. 8vo. 3s. 6d. net. [Sixth Edition.
THE WISE AND THE WAYWARD. Crown 8vo. 6s.
NOTES OF A STRUGGLING GENIUS. Sq. 16mo, wrapper. 1s. net.

Sudermann (H.).
REGINA : OR, THE SINS OF THE FATHERS. A Translation of DER KATZENSTEG. By BEATRICE MARSHALL. Crown 8vo. 6s.

Swettenham (Sir F. A.)
MALAY SKETCHES. Crown 8vo. 6s. [Second Edition.
UNADDRESSED LETTERS. Crown 8vo. 6s.

Syrett (Netta).
NOBODY'S FAULT. Crown 8vo. 3s. 6d. net. [Second Edition.
THE TREE OF LIFE. Crown 8vo. 6s. [Second Edition.

Tabb (John B.).
POEMS. Sq. 32mo. 4s. 6d. net.
LYRICS. Sq. 32mo. 4s. 6d. net.

Taylor (Una),
NETS FOR THE WIND. Crown 8vo. 3s. 6d. net.

Tennyson (Frederick).

POEMS OF THE DAY AND YEAR. Crown 8vo. 5s. net.

Thimm (Carl A.).

A COMPLETE BIBLIOGRAPHY OF FENCING AND DUELLING, AS PRACTISED BY ALL EUROPEAN NATIONS FROM THE MIDDLE AGES TO THE PRESENT DAY. With a Classified Index, arranged Chronologically according to Languages. Illustrated with numerous Portraits of Ancient and Modern Masters of the Art. Title-pages and Frontispieces of some of the earliest works. Portrait of the Author by WILSON STEER. 4to. 21s. net.

Thompson (Francis)

POEMS. With Frontispiece by LAURENCE HOUSMAN. Pott 4to. 5s. net.   [*Fourth Edition.*

SISTER-SONGS: An Offering to Two Sisters. With Frontispiece by LAURENCE HOUSMAN. Pott 4to. 5s. net.

Thoreau (Henry David).

POEMS OF NATURE. Selected and edited by HENRY S. SALT and FRANK B. SANBORN. Fcap. 8vo. 4s. 6d. net.

Traill (H. D.).

THE BARBAROUS BRITISHERS: A Tip-top Novel. Crown 8vo, wrapper. 1s. net.

FROM CAIRO TO THE SOUDAN FRONTIER. Crown 8vo. 5s. net.

Tynan Hinkson (Katharine).

CUCKOO SONGS. Fcap. ,8vo. 5s. net.

MIRACLE PLAYS. OUR LORD'S COMING AND CHILDHOOD. With 6 Illustrations by PATTEN WILSON. Fcap. 8vo. 4s. 6d. net.

Wells (H. G.)

SELECT CONVERSATIONS WITH AN UNCLE, NOW EXTINCT. Fcap. 8vo. 3s. 6d. net.

Walton and Cotton.

THE COMPLEAT ANGLER. Edited by RICHARD LE GALLIENNE. With over 250 Illustrations by EDMUND H. NEW. Fcap. 4to, decorated cover. 15s. net. Also to be had in thirteen 1s. parts.

Warden (Gertrude).

THE SENTIMENTAL SEX. Crown 8vo. 3s. 6d. net.

Watson (H. B. Marriott).

AT THE FIRST CORNER AND OTHER STORIES. Crown 8vo. 3s. 6d. net.

GALLOPING DICK. Crown 8vo. 6s.

THE HEART OF MIRANDA. Crown 8vo. 6s.

Watson (Rosamund Marriott).

VESPERTILIA AND OTHER POEMS. Fcap. 8vo. 4s. 6d. net.

A SUMMER NIGHT AND OTHER POEMS. New Edition. Fcap. 8vo. 3s. net.

Watson (William).

THE FATHER OF THE FOREST AND OTHER POEMS. With New Photogravure Portrait of the Author. Fcap. 8vo. 3s. 6d. net. [*Fifth Thousand.*

ODES AND OTHER POEMS. Fcap. 8vo. 4s. 6d. net. [*Fifth Edition.*

THE ELOPING ANGELS: A Caprice. Square 16mo. 3s. 6d. net. [*Second Edition.*

EXCURSIONS IN CRITICISM: being some Prose Recreations of a Rhymer. Crown 8vo. 5s. net. [*Second Edition.*

THE PRINCE'S QUEST AND OTHER POEMS. Fcap. 8vo. 4s. 6d. net. [*Third Edition.*

THE PURPLE EAST: A Series of Sonnets on England's Desertion of Armenia. With a Frontispiece after G. F. WATTS, R.A. Fcap. 8vo, wrappers. 1s. net. [*Third Edition.*

THE YEAR OF SHAME. With an Introduction by the BISHOP OF HEREFORD. Fcap. 8vo. 2s. 6d. net. [*Second Edition.*

Watson (William)—*cont.*

THE HOPE OF THE WORLD, AND OTHER POEMS. Fcap. 8vo. 3s. 6d. net. [*Third Edition.*

Watt (Francis).

THE LAW'S LUMBER ROOM. Fcap. 8vo. 3s. 6d. net. [*Second Edition.*

THE LAW'S LUMBER ROOM. Second Series. Fcap. 8vo. 4s. 6d. net.

Watts-Dunton (Theodore).

JUBILEE GREETING AT SPITHEAD TO THE MEN OF GREATER BRITAIN. Crown 8vo. 1s. net.

THE COMING OF LOVE AND OTHER POEMS. Crown 8vo. 5s. net. [*Second Edition.*

Wenzell (A. B.)

IN VANITY FAIR. 70 Drawings. Oblong folio. 20s.

Wharton (H. T.)

SAPPHO. Memoir, Text, Selected Renderings, and a Literal Translation by HENRY THORNTON WHARTON. With 3 Illustrations in Photogravure, and a Cover designed by AUBREY BEARDSLEY. With a Memoir of Mr. Wharton. Fcap. 8vo. 6s. net. [*Fourth Edition.*

Wotton (Mabel E.).

DAY BOOKS. Crown 8vo. 3s. 6d. net.

Xenopoulos (Gregory).

THE STEPMOTHER: A TALE OF MODERN ATHENS. Translated by MRS. EDMONDS. Crown 8vo. 3s. 6d. net.

Zola (Emile).

FOUR LETTERS TO FRANCE—THE DREYFUS AFFAIR. Fcap. 8vo, wrapper. 1s. net.

THE YELLOW BOOK

An Illustrated Quarterly.

Pott 4to. 5s. net.

I. April 1894, 272 pp., 15 Illustrations. [*Out of print.*

II. July 1894, 364 pp., 23 Illustrations.

III. October 1894, 280 pp., 15 Illustrations.

IV. January 1895, 285 pp., 16 Illustrations.

V. April 1895, 317 pp., 14 Illustrations.

VI. July 1895, 335 pp., 16 Illustrations.

VII. October 1895, 320 pp., 20 Illustrations.

VIII. January 1896, 406 pp., 26 Illustrations.

IX. April 1896, 256 pp., 17 Illustrations.

X. July 1896, 340 pp., 13 Illustrations.

XI. October 1896, 342 pp., 12 Illustrations.

XII. January 1897, 350 pp., 14 Illustrations.

XIII. April 1897, 316 pp., 18 Illustrations.

TITLES IN THIS SERIES

LIBRARY OF DAVIDSON COLLEGE

Books on regular loan may be checked out for **two weeks**. Books must be presented at the Circulation Desk in order to be renewed.

A fine is charged after date due.

Special books are subject to special regulations at the discretion of the library staff.